"I Won't Be Played With like a Pawn," She Said.

"I don't intend to play with you like a pawn, Evie." Brandon breathed between the sharp, butterfly assaults his lips took upon her throat and the upper planes of her breasts. How had he gotten her like that? "If I 'play' you at all, it will be like a finely tuned instrument. Like a Stradivarius."

Fiercely, he brought her close to him. She was cradled against his chest as his hot mouth devoured hers. He'd won the first battle. Tomorrow's victory in court would be hers.

MARIE NICOLE

is a natural romance writer because her own life has been so romantic. She met her husband-to-be in tenth grade and began dating him in college. The first time he kissed her he made the room fade away, and things have only gotten better for them since.

Dear Reader:

SILHOUETTE DESIRE is an exciting new line of contemporary romances from Silhouette Books. During the past year, many Silhouette readers have written in telling us what other types of stories they'd like to read from Silhouette, and we've kept these comments and suggestions in mind in developing SILHOUETTE DESIRE.

DESIREs feature all of the elements you like to see in a romance, plus a more sensual, provocative story. So if you want to experience all the excitement, passion and joy of falling in love, then SILHOUETTE DESIRE is for you.

Karen Solem
Editor-in-Chief
Silhouette Books

MARIE NICOLE

Tried And True

Published by Silhouette Books New York

America's Publisher of Contemporary Romance

SILHOUETTE BOOKS, a Division of Simon & Schuster, Inc.
1230 Avenue of the Americas, New York, N.Y. 10020

Distributed by Pocket Books

ISBN: 0-671-49195-4

First Silhouette Books printing January, 1984

10 9 8 7 6 5 4 3 2 1

America's Publisher of Contemporary Romance

Printed in the U.S.A.

To Helen Conrad,
with love
and admiration

1

Hello, I'm Brandon Fitzhugh."

"Of course you are."

The dry response was meant to close the little scenario before it even unfolded and send the tall, flamboyant lawyer back to his table at the Miller's-on-Kinzie restaurant, or wherever it was that he had come from.

But he was still standing there, looking not the least bit put off or awkward. Rather, he looked amused, which was the last thing that Yvette Culhane, or Cully, as she was known, wanted.

Brandon turned his wide smile, which was almost blinding against his olive complexion, to the tow-headed boy sitting next to her.

"And this handsome escort is . . . ?" he asked. From anyone else, the words would have sounded stilted and put on. On Brandon's tongue, they sounded natural.

"Tim Culhane," the seven-year-old boy said proudly. It was obvious to Cully that her son instantly liked the broad-shouldered intruder.

"Timmy's my son," Cully heard herself say.

Why was she even bothering to talk to this man? She disliked everything he stood for, and besides, she was going to be facing him in court soon. There was no room for polite chit-chat here—or, more probably, a psyching out on his part.

"How do you do, Tim?" Brandon said, extending his hand to the boy.

Timmy shook it manfully. "Very well, sir," he responded solemnly, his eyes twinkling beneath his bangs.

Brandon looked back toward Cully. "He's got very nice manners," he said easily. "Who taught him?"

His insinuation wasn't wasted on Cully. She raised one brow archly and gave him the coldest look she could muster. "I did," she said crisply. "I've had to teach him everything, since his father walked out on his responsibilities when Timmy was two."

That, she hoped, would put an end to all this "fraternizing." Already she had said more than she was happy about. Cully didn't like to make public things that belonged in her private life.

She hadn't always been that way. Oh, she had been a "scrapper" all her life, as her father had said with only a little pride. But then, as the youngest child, with three older brothers whom she adored, she had had to be. She'd tried to be just like them, and they had egged her on, thinking of her as their personal mascot more than as their kid sister. Her parents had disapproved.

They had also disapproved when Cully refused to follow the die they had cast for her. She didn't care for dolls and was happiest romping with her brothers and playing ball. As time went on, her brothers all turned to the law as their life's work, so Cully turned in that direction, as well.

"If you must go into law, why don't you become a court stenographer?" her father had cried over and over again. "It's more in keeping with your gender."

That had only made Cully try all the harder. She had been Evie in those days, when, despite her drive and determination, she had still harbored a good deal of idealism.

She put herself through school, for her father had refused to contribute to her "folly" in hopes that she would come to her senses and obey his wishes. But she'd had little time for his wishes. She was busy working, studying hard and falling in love. During her first year in law school she met and fell in love with a second year law student, Dick Culhane. He was everything she thought she wanted: blond, engaging and terribly good looking. Having always been considered one of the boys, Cully had been a late bloomer, and it was only then that her classic beauty had come to the fore. Dick Culhane had been the first to notice, and to him she had sold her heart and soul for the price of a wedding ring.

Marriage had brought her nothing but disaster, because they were opposite in every way. While Cully was a dedicated student whose inner drive pushed her to the top of her class, Dick didn't do more than merely coast by. At first he would laugh about it, but soon her drive got in their way. More and more he seemed to resent the time she spent on her studies and the grades she received for them.

When Timmy was born, Dick took that to mean that she would settle down and become "a good little wife and mother." Cully had suddenly realized in horror that Dick was just like her father, wanting her to conform to a subservient role that she just couldn't see herself in.

The beginning of the end came when she passed her bar exam just after he had failed on his third attempt.

"You're more of a man than me, Evie old boy," he had said to her, toasting her with a can of beer in their small apartment.

That had been their only celebration, ending in hot words and secret tears on her part. Timmy had wailed in the background, awakened by the sounds of their shouting.

"If it weren't for the fact that you gave birth to that kid, I'd swear you were a man," Dick had taunted her.

He had left that night, in search, he had told her, of a "real woman," one who didn't feel bent on taking on the whole world to prove herself.

They were divorced shortly thereafter.

Yvette had been lucky enough to land a position in one of Chicago's better known law firms, where she rapidly earned both the respect and acceptance she craved, due to her excellent performance in court. Her nickname had come soon after that. She was far too forceful a person to be addressed as "Yvette," despite the fact that she stood barely five-two in stature and was blessed with both an exceptional figure and beautiful platinum hair, which she wore in a short variation of a pageboy. No, once someone came to know her, "Cully" fitted her much better.

"Mom, can he eat with us?" Timmy asked eagerly, recalling her to the present.

Cully glanced at her son. She realized that it was natural for him to want some sort of male contact in his life. As it was, there were only herself and her Aunt Madge, who lived in an apartment down the hall from them—not much for a boy to build a male image on. Of course, there were his uncles, but, busy with their own lives, they dropped by only infrequently. She'd have to see about getting a "big brother" for him or something, so he wouldn't make these embarrassing demands on her.

"No, Timmy, I'm sure Mr. Fitzhugh has some pressing business to attend to," Cully said, dismissing the suggestion.

"Only eating," Brandon told her innocently.

Cully was surprised at that. Brandon had a reputation of never, ever being without a lovely lady clinging to his arm. To believe that he was actually dining out alone required more of a stretch of the imagination than she was willing to grant. She smelled a rat.

"Then it's okay, Mom?" Timmy asked hopefully.

She had never seen him quite so animated about another person before. It appeared that the fatal Fitzhugh charm, which had made the rounds of courtroom gossip, had struck him down, as well.

Cully searched for a way out. "Well, we're almost half finished, and Mr. Fitzhugh hasn't even ordered yet," she lied. They had hardly begun their dinner.

"That's okay, 'Mom,'" Brandon said. "I'm a fast eater," he promised, his eyes sparkling.

He had blue eyes. Eyes so blue that they might have been fashioned from the sky on a perfect day. Someone had once told her that his charm began with his eyes. The trick was to avoid them. It would have been better to avoid the whole man, but Cully found herself outmaneuvered. But only, she told herself, because she hadn't been ready for a frontal attack. Next time, if there was to be a next time—and she was sure there was, since the case they were involved in was quite newsworthy—she would be more prepared. At the moment, what harm would there be in eating with the man? She wasn't so terribly pliable that she could be taken advantage of just because they had shared a meal.

"With your permission," Brandon said, nodding toward Cully.

"From what I hear, you don't generally ask for permission. You do as you please," she said, trying to indicate that she wasn't sanctioning his joining them, she was merely indifferent to it.

"So do you," he said, waving toward a waiter to bring another chair and place setting.

So he had gone to the trouble of checking her out, had he? Although her five-year career was studded with victories, she had nowhere near the reputation he had, and finding out about her must have taken a little bit of digging on his part. Just how determined was he to undermine her case?

Brandon Fitzhugh had really been brought into her life not by virtue of a "chance" meeting in the Miller's-on-Kinzie restaurant, but because she was the attorney representing Malcolm Woolsey's estate. Malcolm Woolsey had been one of America's golden people, a self-made multimillionaire who refused to put on airs and was as earthy the day he died as he had been while pulling himself up by his boot straps. That was why he and Cully had hit it off so well, although he had originally balked at her being brought in to work with the attorney who was actually handling Woolsey's affairs.

Cully had been determined not to be awed by Woolsey's money or position, and had spoken her mind when he addressed her. She had grown used to battle with her father and the various professors along her route to her diploma, not to mention with the lawyers, mostly male, she had come up against in court. So she was worthy of the war of words. And Woolsey had liked her for it, liked her well enough to invite her to the huge estate on a social level, something he had never done with Harold Taylor, his actual attorney.

That was why, when Harold wound up in the hospital not long after Malcolm Woolsey's death, the head of the firm had told Cully that he had every confidence in the world in her ability to hold down the fort, because trouble was beginning to brew over the will. In it, amid many generous bequests, was the glaring statement that Malcolm did not want any of his money, not even the customary $1.00, going to Serena Woolsey Ashcroft Tennyson, his oldest daughter.

Serena and her father had had a falling out ten years earlier, due to her rebellious, unconventional life-style. He had disowned her then, and time hadn't mellowed his feelings on the matter. She remained disowned and disinherited.

But she didn't accept that quietly. Nothing about the flaming-haired woman was quiet, and her father's body had scarcely cooled before she flew in on her private jet, demanding that her father be declared mentally incompetent and wanting "her share" of the money.

Woolsey's two other children turned to Cully to protect their interests and to carry out their father's wishes. Serena turned to Brandon Fitzhugh, and the battle lines were drawn.

Or so Cully had thought.

"I've declared a cease-fire," Brandon told her as he slipped his tall frame onto the brocaded chair that the waiter produced for him. "I can tell that's on your mind," he told Cully as he perused the menu. "You see, son, your mother and I are going to be facing each other in court," he explained to the attentive boy.

"Are you the rotten shyster that Mom was talking about?" Timmy asked, blurting out what Cully had said to him.

Cully coughed uncomfortably, but Brandon only laughed. His laugh was deep and rich—part of his charm, no doubt, Cully thought, finding it attractive herself, but managing not to show that. Cully had taught herself how to become detached, how to observe things from the sidelines of her own life when she didn't want to become involved.

"Well, Tim, I guess I am," Brandon said. "Unless your Mom's involved in another case with another 'rotten shyster,'" he added, looking over to Cully.

She wished he'd get rid of that amused look on his face. He looked so smug—as if he had all the cards. And he didn't. Even if he *had* won all his cases except for one or two when he was just starting out, Cully meant to beat him. Not just because it would give her own growing career a tremendous boost, what with the media being so involved in the case. And not just for her fee. Cully meant to beat him because he was wrong. Woolsey had been a gruff man, but beneath that, he had been a wounded man, a man who had lavished a great deal of affection and money on a daughter who had grown up to break his heart. And now she was back like the vulture that she was, and Cully was not about to let her have any of Woolsey's money. Perhaps it was foolish, but she felt personally involved in this case.

"You'll have to forgive Timmy. He has a way of being honest—that's also a trait I taught him," Cully said pointedly.

Brandon expressed his approval. "On the contrary, I find it refreshing. There's nothing wrong with honesty," he told her significantly.

Why was he being so agreeable? What was his angle? She had been warned by some of her older colleagues that Brandon could be ruthless and that he always knew how to undermine his opponent far ahead of the actual scene in court.

Yet the handsome, dark-haired man with the incredibly high cheekbones that made him look a little like an Indian seemed nothing less than unassuming charm itself.

That was the most dangerous ploy of all, Cully reckoned. He was going to go after her through her son, she thought suddenly. Well, if that was what he thought, he had another think coming.

"That's a rather strange thing for you to say," Cully said tersely. "From what I hear, your dealings are anything but aboveboard."

Brandon's piercing eyes seemed to size her up

before he bothered making a reply to her statement. "Don't tell me that someone as upstanding as you listens to tacky gossip." He shook his head, then leaned over to Tim and added in a pseudo-whisper, which seemed to please the boy, "I'd never have thought it of her."

"Oh, Mom's okay," Timmy said loftily, coming to her defense in a somewhat left-handed manner.

Brandon looked through the businesslike two-piece gabardine suit Cully wore as if it didn't even exist. His eyes seemed to bore straight through to what was beneath. Cully got the unnerving feeling that he could see down to her pink underwear.

"You bet she is," he said appreciatively.

"I'm sure that those words have been well received every time they've been uttered, Mr. Fitzhugh, but I'm afraid they won't wash here," Cully said in her best lawyer tones.

"I've just given the lady a compliment, not a basket of dirty laundry," he said to Timmy, who giggled at the joke. Brandon raised his eyes to look at Cully. "Your son seems to have a sense of humor. Is that also something you've taught him?" Cully didn't answer. "If so, I think you might do with a refresher course yourself," he advised gently.

"I could do with dinner in peace," she said tensely, not liking the way things were going at all.

Brandon cocked his head endearingly. The lights in the restaurant all seemed to play off his almost perfect, chiseled profile. All the stories of his romantic escapades raced through Cully's mind. The big oaf. He was probably proud of his overbearing sexual prowess. Well, it wouldn't work here. She'd been exposed to his type before, men who were nothing but chauvinistic bigots and always ended up surprised at being outmaneuvered by a woman. Brandon Fitzhugh would learn his lesson by and by, she thought, and that heartened her enough that she allowed a smile to curve her lips.

"War hasn't been declared," he told her softly.

"Oh, hasn't it?" she countered. "You're on the opposite side," she reminded him.

"But nowhere in my lawyers' manual does it say I have to duel to the death for a client. Besides, I'm not here to talk shop talk," he informed her genially. "And I like your smile. Makes you look almost . . ." He paused, as if for effect, she thought. ". . . soft," he ended.

She held her head up high. "Well, I'm not," she told him almost proudly. Soft women got trampled on and had their hearts torn out, she mentally added.

"Your mom a robot?" he asked Timmy, who giggled once more and shook his head so hard that his hair swung back and forth in front of his eyes. Brandon looked back at Cully. "He says you're soft."

"Just why are you here?" she asked, challenging him. She'd had enough of this word-play.

"To eat," he told her, looking around. "That is, if the waiter ever comes back."

As if on cue, the somberly dressed waiter appeared, ready to take Brandon's order.

Cully began to eat hurriedly, not wanting to spend any more time in Brandon's company than was absolutely necessary.

"Hey, Mom, slow down. Mr. Fitzhugh's gonna be left all alone with his meal," Timmy protested, obviously not about to let go of his newfound friend so quickly.

The fact that he was using her child angered Cully no end. "That's the idea, Timmy," she said, but she was looking at Brandon when she said it.

"You see, Tim," Brandon said confidentially as his salad arrived, "your mom's a terrific lawyer, but they tell me she's lacking in some social graces."

"And just who are 'they'?" Cully wanted to know, putting down her fork dramatically.

"People," Brandon said vaguely. "People who see things—and talk."

"You seem to have gone to an awful lot of trouble to find things out about me," she said coldly.

"I like to know my opposition," Brandon said simply as he cut appreciatively into the prime rib that had just arrived.

Above a good woman and a good victory, Brandon liked a good meal. Someone had once said that about him in passing and it now came back to Cully. Funny how much information she had accumulated about him without ever meeting him. But she was good at that, good at amassing and retaining myriads of details for future use. That was why the bar exam had been such a breeze for her. Remembering different court cases had never been a problem for her. Dealing with people, though, had. She had lost her open friendliness when her husband had walked out on her. She had thought of him as the man she wanted to spend forever with, and when she had turned out to be so wrong she had pulled back from people altogether, dealing with them on a work level only—until she had met Malcolm Woolsey, who, despite his cantankerous nature, had become her friend in a short time.

"Does that include tailing your opposition?" she asked.

"Although I'm sure you have a most lovely tail, if the rest of you is any indication," he said with an easy smile that utterly unnerved her, "this meeting is quite by happenstance. A very fortuitous happenstance," he told her.

"I know your opinion of women, Mr. Fitzhugh," Cully said, her now unwanted dinner growing cold.

"Oh, do you now?" he asked engagingly.

"And I don't fit into any of your preset categories," she informed him.

"Let's start a new category, then," he proposed obligingly.

"Will you stop being cute and let me finish?" she demanded, her temper threatening to flare, which annoyed her even further. She never let go of her temper. Damn him. Five minutes in his presence, and she was losing the battle.

"Why, Miss Culhane—"

"Ms.," she corrected.

"—you flatter me," he said, flashing a smile of pretended embarrassment.

"What?" The man was crazy. She had heard that he was unorthodox, but this was utterly ridiculous.

"Calling me cute," he clarified. "Of course, the word *handsome* has come up in connection with my name, but never *cute*," he said, keeping a straight face, although his eyes gave him away.

Cully bit her lip, trying to regroup. If he won there, what was going to happen in court? "Mr. Fitzhugh—"

"Brandon," he insisted.

"Mr. Fitzhugh," she repeated purposely, "I know all about your out-of-court tactics."

"And they are?" he asked, gazing into her eyes.

"Psyching out and unnerving your opponents," she said triumphantly.

"You make it sound as if we were in the Olympics," he said, his smile unruffled.

"Your term, not mine," she said tersely, indicating that, even so, it was her term as well. "And I won't be psyched out. You can go back to your voluptuous client and tell her that this time your tactics won't work."

"Mom, why are you shouting?" Timmy asked, dismayed.

"Yes, 'Mom,' why are you shouting?" Brandon asked beguilingly. "I came in under a white flag of truce—" he began innocently.

"Why?" she demanded, her green eyes burning with sparks of liquid fire. His answer was bound to make Timmy see what kind of a man he was.

"To meet a lovely lady and her young escort," he said, saving his smile for Timmy, who responded in kind.

She knew that her son heard only the obvious meanings of words. If she did anything right then, she would be the heavy in his eyes. For the moment she simply took a deep breath.

"Ah, that seems to have left you speechless. I must make a note of that." He pulled out a little black notebook and proceeded to write saying the words aloud at the same time, "Call her lovely just as the trial starts and you've got it made." He looked up at her, putting his notebook back in his jacket pocket. "Psyched out yet?" he asked.

"No!" she retorted.

"Good. I like nothing better than a good court fight . . . and a good dinner." His eyes lighted on her, and the look in them didn't match his words. He appeared to be thinking something entirely different. "Do you think we could have one sometime?"

"If we're not having it now," Cully said, "we're not going to have it at all." The waiter came by to inquire whether she was finished with her meal, and Cully nodded at him. He swept away her almost full plate and returned with dessert.

"Tim, do you think you could talk your mom into going out with me sometime?" Brandon asked, lowering his voice to the level of a fellow conspirator.

Cully straightened as if she had been given an electrical shock. "You don't need a go-between," she informed Brandon stiffly.

"I don't?" he asked with a wide smile.

"No, I can tell you directly myself. No. I do not eat out with . . . with . . ."

"Men?" he asked, helpfully supplying the word for her. "Present company excepted, of course," he said smilingly to Tim, who reacted in kind.

"No, I was thinking of the word *chauvinists,*" Cully said. Why was he twisting everything so neatly against her in front of her most precious audience? She hated him.

"Why am I a chauvinist?" Brandon wanted to know. "Because I said you were beautiful?"

"You didn't say that," she said sharply, annoyed that he could think she'd fall for such a ploy.

"Oh, well, then you have a reason to be angry. I should have said it. You are," he told her, his voice soft and low.

That was all she could stand of this overbearing egotist. She rose. "Timmy," she said in a commanding voice, "let's go."

"Aw, but, Mom, I haven't finished my ice cream," the boy protested, looking not at his unfinished dessert, but at Brandon.

"I'll buy you a cone," Cully said. "I'll buy you a whole half gallon." She took his hand in hers. "We're going. Since you've ruined my meal, Mr. Fitzhugh," she said with controlled anger, "you can pay for it."

And with that Yvette Culhane left Brandon alone at the table with his prime ribs.

2

The drive home in the taxi was short.

When she found herself having difficulty paying attention to what her son was saying, Cully realized that Brandon's sudden appearance at the restaurant had disturbed her more than she had thought. The relationship between mother and son was a close one, despite Cully's heavy work load and all the hours she devoted to her cases. She always found time, no matter how busy she was, to listen to him and to try to take part in his life. She did her best to be both mother and father to him, becoming knowledgeable in all sorts of sports so that he would never lack for a "sports buddy" to talk things over with.

But the way he had lit up when that loathesome man talked to him told Cully that there was still an empty space in the little boy's life, and try as she might, she couldn't fill it. The thought of getting

Timmy a "big brother" came back to her. She had considered it once before, but had cast the idea aside because it would mean allowing a man to come into her home, if only in passing. And Cully was quite against that. She still smarted too much from all her battles, whether with Dick, her father, or the many men who seemed determined to regard her as only a fluffy little woman. The fact that she was so blond and petite didn't help any. She had to struggle twice as hard to convince them that she was indeed serious about being both a lawyer and in total control of her life. She didn't want to be taken care of.

Of course, there had been times when it would have been nice to surrender the mantle of protector and controller—like the time when Timmy had an accident and she spent two days in the hospital at his side, not knowing if he were going to live or die. It would have been nice to have had a man's shoulder to cry on then. But her stubbornness had seen her through with her chin held high, and when her father had come along to lend his moral support, something within Cully had fought against it and made her say that she was all right and handling everything just fine.

Cully doubted if she knew how to accept help anymore. She was too used to doing everything on her own. But still, the fact remained that Timmy needed some sort of male influence in his life. If her brothers only had more time, that would solve everything. But Alex and Teddy had families of their own, and Pete was busy making a name for himself and having a ball as a bachelor. Besides, she thought, they should volunteer their time. She didn't want to go begging, not even for Timmy. So getting Timmy a "big brother" was the only alternative. She couldn't let her own prejudices and bad experiences lead her to deprive her son.

"What are you thinking about, Mom?" Timmy's high voice broke into the middle of her thoughts.

"Hmm?" She looked at him fondly, tousling his hair.

"You're not listening to me," Timmy pointed out.

"I'm sorry, darling. I was just thinking," she confessed. They had always been honest with one another, and she wasn't about to tell him that she had heard every word that he had said when she hadn't.

"About that man?" he asked eagerly.

"What man?" she said, her brows coming together.

"Mr. Fitzhugh," Timmy said with a touch of impatience. "What other man do you think?"

"No, I wasn't thinking about him," she said in a dismissive tone. "I've got better things to think about —like you," she said, a smile coming back to her face.

"Me?" he asked, his green eyes dancing. "Is it something good?" he wanted to know.

"I think so," she said with affection. "I was thinking —right here, driver," she said, suddenly realizing that they were home.

The driver pulled over to the curb. Cully fished out the right amount, plus a tip, then stepped out. Her high heels clicked smartly on the concrete as she walked toward their building. It was a pleasant spring evening, and she thought for a moment of going for a walk with Timmy, peering into the windows of the little shops that lined both sides of the city street. But it was getting late, and she had a lot of work to do the next day. There was that meeting with the Woolseys . . .

"You were thinking . . ." Timmy prompted, tugging at her jacket sleeve.

Once more she pulled her thoughts together as she looked down at her son, taking his arm. "I was thinking that maybe I'd look into the idea of getting you a big brother."

"You're gonna get married?" Timmy asked, his light eyebrows rising and getting lost beneath the broad fringe of his blond hair.

"No, silly, I mean the kind they have on those TV commercials. Some man who'd do boy things with you," she said as they walked past the doorman and into the foyer of the eight-year-old apartment building. The elevator was right there, so they didn't have to wait.

"How about Mr. Fitzhugh?" he asked as the elevator door closed.

"Certainly not!" Cully said, annoyed at the very thought; then her expression softened. "Why on earth would you want him?" she asked, deciding to explore the ridiculous thought and, by dissecting it, lay it to rest forever.

"He seems like a real neat guy," Timmy told her.

"Well, he's not. Take it from me." The expression on Timmy's face faded a little. They came to their floor and walked out onto the freshly shampooed mauve rug that ran the length of the long hallway. "When you get a little older," she promised, "you'll understand about things like that."

Timmy shrugged. "He seemed like a nice man," he persisted.

"That, my friend, is part of his combat training," she said as she fished out her key.

"Huh?"

"Never mind, I'll explain it all to you later," she said.

"When I'm fifty," Timmy muttered dejectedly.

"Naw—when you're forty-nine," she said, keeping a straight face. Then they both laughed. "Hi, Aunt Madge—oh, it came!" she exclaimed, having barely greeted her aunt before her eyes fell on the teak server that stood against the far wall, demanding her inspection.

Cully walked over to it and ran her fingers along the intricate carvings that covered the entire bar. It was her newest acquisition for her oriental-style living room.

"It came about an hour ago, but I thought I'd stick around and finish this," the pleasant, round-faced woman said, nodding toward the romance novel she had just put down. She struggled to get out of the chair she'd been sitting in. It took a bit of an effort, because the cushion was very soft and Madge was rather wide, given to sinking in comfortably.

"I'm sorry to have inconvenienced you," Cully apologized. "They were supposed to have come earlier—and I did promise Timmy dinner out."

Madge waved her hand, dismissing the apology. "I had nothing special doing," she told her niece. "Besides, those delivery men were cute," she said, a bit of a sparkle dancing in her eyes. "Maybe you should have stuck around."

"Madge," Cully said patiently, but affectionately, because she knew that her aunt only meant well, "I have no use for men, cute or otherwise, in my life. My career and my son are enough for me."

"No woman is complete without a man," Madge insisted.

Cully arched an amused brow. "Be nice to me or I'll report you to the women's movement," she warned.

Madge shook her henna-colored, fluffy hair, which encircled her head like a wayward halo. "Every woman needs a man in her life," she persisted. "I had my Jonathan for thirty years, and with him gone, I'm out there looking for someone like him," she pointed out.

"Maybe that's my trouble," Cully said in a voice that was slightly lower in order not to attract Timmy's keen attention. The boy was busy exploring the server, exposing nooks and crannies where glasses and bottles could be stored. "I never had a good man in my life to make me want any others," she said with a trace of bitterness.

"Well, you're never going to get one if you keep hiding under rocks," Madge said, crossing her ample arms before her even more ample chest.

"I do not hide under rocks, and I do not want to go into this tonight," Cully said in a no-nonsense voice that still managed not to be cold. She knew just how to word things in a way that wouldn't hurt her aunt, but would still indicate that she had had quite enough of the subject.

"Oh, I picked up your mail for you," Madge said, suddenly recalling the fact. "Here." She shoved one envelope extra hard toward Cully.

To appease the woman, Cully opened it first. It was an ad for a computer dating service. Cully looked at Madge, who shrugged her shoulders innocently.

"Well, it wouldn't hurt to fill it in," the older woman pointed out.

Cully clutched at her chest. "Oh, the pain of it," she cried, pretending to be wounded.

Madge threw up her hands in temporary defeat. "All right, all right, I'll retreat—for now. But you mark my words; there's a man out there for you somewhere, Evie, and you can't hide from him forever," she said, shaking a stubby finger.

Cully smiled, kissing the woman's forehead. Madge was just as short as she was, but preferred to wear flat-heeled shoes, so she appeared shorter. "Well, if he's out there, there's no point in filling this out and messing things up, is there?" she asked, tearing up the ad.

"How was your dinner?" Madge asked, finding it best to switch to another subject.

Timmy looked up brightly. "We met this real nice guy," he told the woman, his eyes darting over to his mother.

"We met Brandon Fitzhugh," Cully corrected in a flat tone.

Madge looked at her curiously. "Why do you make it sound like those are two contradictory statements?" she asked.

"Because Brandon Fitzhugh is a snake in the grass who uses every means available to him to win," she said.

"Isn't that what the lawyer game is all about? Winning?" Madge asked, apparently confused.

"No, it's about honesty and integrity," Cully insisted.

"And winning," Madge injected.

"*If* you're right," Cully said more firmly.

"You're too pure for my tastes, kid," Madge said, shaking her head. "If you don't win, you don't pay for that little doohickey there," she said casually, pointing to the server. "And five hundred little Buddhist nuns would have worked their fingers to the bone for nothing."

"Buddhists don't have nuns," Cully corrected with a grin.

Madge shrugged. "Whatever."

"I'm not saying that winning isn't important," Cully said patiently. "I'm just saying that Brandon Fitzhugh's ways are all wrong. He relies on dramatics and emotion in the court and . . . well, the juries are always at least half women—"

"Aha!" Madge said, coming in closer. "Now we're getting to it."

Cully whirled around, on the alert. "Getting to what?" she asked defensively.

Madge turned to Timmy. "Timmy, tell your old Aunt Madge what this guy looks like," she urged.

"Madge, that has nothing to do with anything!" Cully protested, but Madge waved at her to be quiet.

"Well?" she asked Timmy encouragingly, stooping down to his level.

Timmy closed the door he had been experimenting with and thought for a moment. "Kind of like Superman—except in a suit," he said.

"Like Clark Kent?" Madge asked helpfully.

Timmy shook his head. "No, not like that. Clark Kent is kinda dopey-looking. Mr. Fitzhugh isn't dopey. I like the way he talks," Timmy confided.

Madge cast a knowing eye back at Cully. "So he's a knockout, is he?"

Cully shrugged. "He's not bad-looking."

"From you, that's a testimonial."

"Madge, the man is a con artist," Cully insisted heatedly. "His methods are unorthodox. Why, he tried to wheedle his way into Timmy's affections just because I'm going to be facing him in court soon."

"Come again?" Madge asked, rising to her feet again somewhat awkwardly.

Cully pulled her aside. "The Woolsey case. His daughter turned up out of the blue and is contesting the will. He's representing her."

"So?"

"So, for no reason at all, he turned up at the restaurant this evening." Didn't Madge see the connection?

"Man's gotta eat," she said in his defense.

"Madge, there are scores of restaurants in Chicago. Why did he pick Miller's-on-Kinzie?" she wanted to know.

"You've got similar tastes?" Madge offered with a shrug.

"No, a simpler explanation is that he's following me," she told the older woman.

"Even better!" Madge said brightly, beaming. "You could do worse than have Superman following you."

"Will you listen?" Cully cried desperately. "He's following me to try to get to me, unnerve me. If he's Timmy's friend, maybe I, as a 'typical woman,'" she said the term disparagingly, "will have second thoughts about going for broke and beating him in court. He's trying to psych me out by using Timmy against me," she insisted.

"Maybe you'd better stop reading those mysteries all the time," Madge advised. "Here." She pushed her romance novel toward Cully. "Try this for a change."

Cully pushed the book back. "I know what I'm saying. This isn't a mystery plot; it's just the way he operates. Listen, I'm going to change into something more comfortable; stay awhile if you like," Cully said, heading for the bedroom. "As long as you promise not to talk about men or romance," she added.

Madge shook her head. "What else is there?" she wanted to know.

"Madge," Cully called out from the bedroom as she took off her smart, peach business suit and slipped into a kimono, tying it tightly about her slim waist, "there are countless other topics."

"None of them interesting," Madge said dismissively.

The doorbell rang just then.

"You expecting anyone—or anything—else? Maybe a samurai sword?" she asked.

"No," Cully laughed. "Will you get that? I'll be right out," she said, running a brush through her hair and letting it fall softly about her face. She looked far less businesslike now, far less the no-nonsense lawyer she portrayed in the work world, she thought with a small smile on her lips as she looked into the mirror. But this was a side of her that only Timmy and Madge saw. There was no need for a protective shield with them.

She came out of her room and into the living room just as Madge opened the door. Cully had just stepped past the black silk screen that half covered the entrance from the hall into the living room when she heard Timmy exclaim, "Mr. Fitzhugh!"

"Well, hello, Superman," Madge said, obvious admiration in her voice as she looked at the man.

In the doorway, holding what appeared to be a shopping bag heavily filled with something or other, stood Brandon Fitzhugh.

"I beg your pardon?" he asked, looking down at Madge. His easy smile looked a trifle perplexed as well as amused. "I'm looking for Yvette Culhane," he told her, already grinning at Timmy.

"Come on in," Madge said, taking a good grip on his forearm and almost pulling him in.

"What do you want?" Cully asked in an icy voice once her initial shock had faded. Timmy was already excitedly greeting the tall interloper.

"Hi, Tiger," Brandon said, nodding to Timmy. "Is this your sister?" he asked, smiling at Madge.

Madge apparently knew that Brandon was being deliberately, even cold-bloodedly, charming, but she also apparently didn't care, because she seemed to bloom at the comment. "No, I'm Evie's aunt," she said, her brown eyes sweeping over Brandon in a quick assessment.

Cully could tell immediately what was on Madge's mind, and she knew that she had to save herself before it was too late. "I said, what do you want?" Cully demanded, folding her arms in front of her. The long sleeves of the pink and white kimono hid the tips of her fingers as she did so.

"To make amends," he said innocently.

"You can do that by leaving," Cully told him in no uncertain terms.

"Evie, where're your manners?" Madge asked, making Cully all the more angry. He had her family siding against her, and she disliked being reprimanded in front of him.

"That's all right, Mrs. . . ." Brandon's voice trailed off as he waited for Madge to fill in the space.

"It's Monahan, but you can call me Madge," the

older woman told him brightly, her sparkling eyes clearly indicating that she had taken an instant liking to the handsome man.

There was little not to like, appearance-wise. He was tall, with an olive complexion, and filled out his suit like a tailor's dream: broad-shouldered with a flat stomach, tapering hips and perfectly well rounded buttock muscles. He looked like an athlete in training. Cully wondered when he got time for any exercise other than his legendary bed romps, which had been the source of spicy gossip for a long time.

"Madge, then," he said graciously with a slight cocking of his head, making him look like an endearing but mischievous little boy. Cully was willing to bet that he had always managed to get away with a lot, knowing just how to worm his way in and out of things by virtue of his charm and those eyes of his. "I'm afraid your niece does have a point against me."

"Why?" Madge asked, sounding as if she were ready to come to his aid.

"Well, I ruined her dinner, I'm afraid," Brandon said in confidential tones.

"How?" Madge asked incredulously.

"By showing up, it seems," Brandon said, now looking at Cully.

Cully could see the light of pleasure in his eyes as he took in her appearance. She realized that she was standing before him in her kimono, with only her bra and half slip on beneath it, and she felt rather ill at ease, as if she had been stripped of her armor. She hated him for the sudden, vulnerable feeling he awoke, and her anger at his intrusion grew to irrational proportions. She hated feeling at a disadvantage, which she knew was exactly his game. So far, he was winning.

"Now, how could that be?" Madge asked in disbelief. If Cully didn't know better, she would have said that her aunt was flirting. Brandon had that kind of an effect on women.

Brandon merely shrugged his broad shoulders, the powder blue suit moving with the motion as if it was one with him. "I'm afraid I killed her appetite."

"Don't pay Evie any mind," Madge said apologetically. "She's got this sharp tongue."

"Madge!" Cully cried, annoyed.

"Hey, I'm beginning to leak," Brandon said, and Cully stared at him. "The bag," he explained, putting his hand under it to keep the paper from giving way. "I brought Chinese food," he told her.

"Well, don't just stand there, get some plates," Madge directed.

Cully did as she was told, glancing at Brandon over her shoulder. He followed her into the kitchen, which was done all in earth tones. Madge and Timmy trooped in after them.

"Why Chinese food?" Cully asked sharply.

"Because it's your favorite," Brandon replied simply.

This was worse than she thought. He had gone through an awful lot of trouble to find things out about her. Serena must really be paying beyond the call of duty for his services. Either that, or he really hated losing.

Brandon moved to put the endangered bag on the counter, and not a moment too soon. The frail paper on the bottom gave way, letting the carton of fried rice land with a thud.

"How did you know that?" Cully wanted to know, slowly opening the bag while she watched his face.

"A good lawyer knows everything," he told her with a smile. It looked totally guileless and was thus even more unsettling.

"Well, the two of you have a lot to talk about, so I'll just be going," Madge said obligingly, beginning to leave the kitchen.

"No!" Cully cried. She didn't want to be alone with this man, not until she was sure of her ground—and definitely not in her kimono. His reputation made that far too dangerous a situation, even with Timmy home.

"No," Brandon said easily, almost at the same time. "I brought enough for a small army. I was really trying to make amends, and I wasn't sure just what Chinese food you liked," he told Cully, then looked back at Madge. "There's more than enough for you."

"Well . . ." Madge considered, looking torn between her appetite and her desire to play Cupid.

"You'll stay," Cully said firmly, drawing an extra stool up to the counter in the breakfast nook. "This is for you, Mr. Fitzhugh," she said, setting his place at the far end of the counter. "Timmy, you're here," she said. "Then Madge. And I'll take the end stool," she finished, placing herself next to the wall for safety's sake.

Brandon eyed her with amusement, but said nothing as he slid onto his assigned seat. He seemed perfectly content to share his company with Timmy and carried on a conversation with the boy easily. First tactical mistake, Cully thought grimly.

Cully spent the next forty-five minutes in relative

silence, listening to Brandon charm the pants off Madge and Timmy and wondering how on earth she had gotten herself into this position. There was nothing written, but there had to be something highly unethical about all this camaraderie. Well, she'd let him think that he was trimming her sails, taking the fighting edge off her by showing these "wonderful traits" of his. She was surprised he hadn't shown up with a faithful dog at his heels.

All this wasn't going to do him one bit of good. She knew him for what he truly was: a dirty fighter. And even if he wasn't, even if he had been her own brother, she'd go up against him fighting to win, fighting with every available piece of evidence at her disposal.

She looked at him over the bent heads of her aunt and her son, an amused smile on her own lips. It was all so terribly obvious. The poor man was knocking himself out for no reason. She was too smart for him, she thought.

Brandon turned his head in her direction, as if he sensed her watching him, and he smiled. It was a smile women dreamed about and dentists shuddered over, she thought fleetingly. Every tooth in that head was straight, white and perfect. Everything else looked perfect, too. No wonder he considered himself a free-lance Casanova. If face value was all there was to go on, Brandon Fitzhugh was certainly at the head of his class.

And his brilliant blue eyes said wonderful things to her, things that had no place in their present situation. Well, if he was looking to woo her, he was going to meet with quite a surprise, she thought to herself. The thought pleased her a great deal.

She met his gaze head on, refusing either to look down first or smile invitingly. It was a look, she felt, that said, "I know what you're all about and you're not fooling me."

Yet Brandon didn't look put off in the least.

3

Somewhere between the lichee chicken and the fortune cookies, Madge deserted Cully.

"You can't leave," Cully whispered as she followed the older woman to the door, trying to persuade the older woman to stay.

"Hold on to this one, Evie," Madge said, patting Cully's hand.

"There's nothing to hold on to," Cully insisted. "He's only here because he has an ulterior motive."

A funny smile passed over Madge's lips. "Hold out a little," she advised, looking at the kimono with a fairly dreamy look, "before you give in to the ulterior motive." There was a twinkle in her eye when she finished; she left before Cully had a chance to stop her.

This was getting entirely out of hand, Cully thought, turning around slowly. From the kitchen, she heard sounds of laughter. He had completely infiltrated her poor son's unsuspecting heart, and that was more than she would put up with. She marched back into the kitchen, the kimono shaping and reshaping itself about her body as she moved quickly.

The sight of her son looking so happy took her aback for a moment. He seemed to thrive on a male relationship, the one thing she couldn't give him. She resented Brandon even more.

Brandon looked up as she reentered, his eyes smiling. "Tim tells me you're thinking of getting him a 'big brother,'" he said, toying with his fortune cookie. "I'd say that's a very good idea."

The smile she gave him back was stiff and formal. "Thank you, but I really wasn't waiting with bated breath for your approval on the matter. Timmy, you know better than to discuss private matters with strangers," she chided.

The boy looked up at her innocently. "But he's not a stranger, Mom. Brandon's—"

"We're not going to get that familiar," she told her son unyieldingly. "It's Mr. Fitzhugh."

"Now, the boy meant no harm," Brandon told her, something about his manner taking authority away from her. "I told him to call me Brandon. Besides, you can't call someone who brings you moo goo gai pan a stranger. In some countries that would be grounds for an engagement."

Cully looked down at her son. "Timmy, it's time to go to bed," she said sharply. What she had to say to this . . . this oaf she'd say in private. She didn't want her son to see her lose her temper.

Timmy's face fell and he actually looked toward Brandon in appeal.

"Better do as your mom says, Tim. She knows best," Brandon advised kindly.

"I can manage my son without your help," she snapped testily. "Timmy?" she said expectantly. Timmy slid off his stool and kissed her good night a bit reluctantly.

"Will I see you again?" he asked Brandon.

"No," Cully said firmly.

But Brandon merely smiled. "Sure," he said. "Good night, Tiger."

Timmy went off to bed happily, leaving a very unhappy Cully in his wake. She turned on Brandon, looking at him accusingly. "You shouldn't lie to him like that."

"I wasn't lying," Brandon told her, his voice dropping a few decibels so it sounded sultry and warm. Here comes stage two, Cully thought, bracing herself for the attack.

"Yes, you were, because you're never going to be here again," she informed him, clearing away the dishes quickly. To her surprise and dismay, he joined her, scraping off the remains into the separate little cartons and closing them, then stacking the dishes in the sink faster than she could, even though she tried to get everything out of his way. She didn't want him helping her.

"I'd hate to think of our beautiful relationship as being over so quickly," Brandon said, his voice sexy and languid.

Cully's eyes shot fire. What did he think she was, some simpleton? She spun away from the sink so fast that her belt came undone and the kimono floated open, exposing her soft, pink lingerie. With angry hands she quickly retied the sash, all too aware of the look of admiration that passed over Brandon's face as he took in the view of her breasts, full and barely hidden behind the nylon bra.

"We have no beautiful relationship, Mr. Fitzhugh!"

"The evening is young—" he reminded her.

"But the lines are old," she interrupted. "And I was not born yesterday," she told him, rinsing off the dishes that he insisted on handing her.

"It would make me a cradle robber if you were," he responded, totally undaunted.

She put down the dish towel she had picked up. "Look, you have a reputation—"

"All lies," he assured her innocently, his eyes rolling up. It was almost comical, and she wanted to laugh . . . would have laughed if he hadn't been who he was.

"—and I know all your ploys," she went on doggedly.

"I'm flattered," he said. "You've studied me."

"Don't be flattered," she told him. "Just be gone."

But he made no move toward the door. Instead he looked around. "Does that beautiful piece of furniture harbor any Scotch bottles?" he wanted to know, walking out into the living room and looking at her newest purchase.

"I'm throwing you out of my house," she cried in confusion, spreading her hands helplessly as she followed him out. "How can you be asking for a drink?"

"Because I'm thirsty," he said simply. Then his gaze slowly inched its way down her body. "And talking to beautiful women makes me thirstier."

The way he said it, she wasn't all that sure he was merely talking about a drink anymore.

"Now, I've heard that the tigress of the courtroom is at least mildly hospitable, or is that as much of a lie as my reputation is?" he asked, his eyebrow arched, waiting.

Cully marched over to her old bar, pulled down a bottle of Scotch and poured two fingers. Never had a drink been given so grudgingly, she thought as she shoved it into his hand.

"Number one, no one ever called me the tigress of the courtroom, and I resent your condescension—"

"I—"

"Number two," she continued, talking over his voice until he merely sat down on the loveseat, letting her go on. "I am hospitable—to people I invite into my house, not gate-crashers. And number three, your reputation, both as an overly flamboyant, devious lawyer and as a womanizer, is indeed merited," she said sarcastically, looking down at him accusingly.

He raised his hand. "The defense would like its turn now before the last nail is put into the coffin," he told her. "Once I take on a client, I do everything I can to win for them. That's why they hire me. No one hires a lawyer to lose for them," he pointed out, taking a sip of his drink. His voice was a trifle more serious. "And number two, I am not a womanizer." Cully opened her mouth, but this time, he wouldn't let her cut in. "A womanizer uses women. I do not use, I enjoy. That's what we're all down here for, to enjoy one another—and life—as best we can, and you, lady, have forgotten that, if you ever knew it at all."

Cully's hands went to her hips as her green eyes narrowed to angry slits. "Don't you preach at me!" she exclaimed. "I know perfectly well how to enjoy life!" she informed him.

He put down his drink and looked up at her, more than a trace of the devil in his eyes. "Do you, now?" he asked.

What happened next was entirely unforseen, at least by Cully. When later she played it back in her head over and over, looking it over from every angle, she had to admit that she had been totally unprepared. He grabbed her wrist and pulled her down onto his lap, kissing her horrified mouth with more enthusiasm than just one half finished glass of Scotch could have produced.

She beat on his back with her fists, demanding to be released from his strong grip, but she couldn't squirm out of his lap. Something totally unbidden and new seemed to flower right in the middle of her stomach, light years away from her conscious being. An explosion, ever so tiny, went off.

She glared at him when he did release her. In one swift motion her hand flew out, leaving an angry red blotch on his cheek. He hardly seemed to feel it. It was almost as if he had expected it.

"That's hardly enjoying life," he pointed out.

Cully pointed toward the door. "Get out of here!" she demanded. "Get out of here right now!" she told him.

He rose slowly, taking his time. All the while his hypnotic eyes held on to that part of her being that had just fluttered into existence. "Okay—for now," he told her.

"Mr. Fitzhugh," she said, digging into her reserves for a calm that she did not feel, "if you come here again I will have you forcibly removed."

"I'd enjoy a wrestling match," he said, his body so

close to hers that it almost touched. A spark of electricity jumped through her. What was going on here? her mind demanded. Was she actually physically attracted to this Neanderthal?

"By the police," she added, angered more at her own involuntary response to him than at his words.

His eyes twinkled. "What are you afraid of?" he wanted to know.

That was the last straw. "I am not *afraid* of you, Mr. Fitzhugh. I am *repulsed* by you and everything you stand for," she informed him.

"You have no idea," he said mysteriously, still baiting her, "what it is I stand for."

"Don't try to change my mind," she warned. "You're highly unethical—"

"Oh, no, so far I've been terribly ethical. Want to see me get unethical?" he offered mischievously, taking her into his arms. She struggled against him, unhappy about the effect that being pressed against his body was having on her. It was as if her body and mind were suddenly totally detached from each other. She hadn't made love to a man since Dick had left her. Was this a cry for fulfillment of a basic need? She would die before she'd let that need be fulfilled by Brandon and become one of "Brandon's Beautiful Babies," as his collection of lady friends was referred to by competing lawyers with pot bellies and envious minds.

"No!" she cried, but he kissed her again. This time, even as her hands desperately tried to push him away, that flowering something within her grew a little larger, a little greedier, savoring the sweet taste of his warm lips upon hers just the tiniest bit more. With a forceful resolve surging through her, Cully brought back her foot and let loose with a kick to his shin, trying mightily to save herself.

"Ow!" he yelled, releasing her and hopping back.

Cully stood before him, tossing her head back triumphantly. "You deserve worse than that!" she told him. She realized that she was breathing more heavily than she would have liked. He had really rattled her nerves, the louse!

Brandon eyed her for a moment, as if thinking things through and trying to keep his temper in check. She had expected him to walk out in a huff, slamming the door behind him. But he was still there, still regarding her with eyes that were dissecting both her and whatever inner thoughts he was having.

"You're a feisty one," he finally said. "And I'm not quite sure what there is about you that attracts me," he added softly.

Didn't he ever give up? "Other than my gorgeous face, my well-turned figure and sparkling personality?" Cully asked sarcastically. "It's probably your insatiable lust for women. Well, you're not scoring tonight, Mr. Fitzhugh, on any front," she said, getting around him and manfully trying to push him out the door. "And when we meet in court, I'm going to cut your heart out!" she promised.

She could never have moved him on her own, but she hoped that her final gesture would get him to leave, and it did. He stood in her doorway, a smile on his face. He tried to run a finger over her lips, and Cully pulled her head back with a pronounced jerk. "We'll see about that," he said, as if he didn't believe her threat, which heightened her annoyance all the more. "I'll be calling you," he promised.

"I won't be answering," she replied flippantly.

"I'd like to take you out to dinner some night—just the two of us," he persisted.

"No," she retorted. He was unbelievable. How thick was his head?

"Why?" he asked. "I know for a fact that you eat," he said, nodding toward the kitchen area.

"Not with egotistical maniacs," she told him.

"Fine, I won't invite any," he promised.

"You couldn't find any," she said cryptically. "Compared to you, they're all shy and retiring!"

He merely laughed. "You ate with me tonight, and you didn't want to. You kissed me tonight, and you didn't want to—or so you said," he added devilishly. "We'll see, Pussycat," he said with a wink. "We'll see."

Since words didn't seem to do the trick, Cully decided the next best thing was to slam the door in his face. And she did. Then she leaned against it, half expecting him to try to force his way back in. But he didn't. Of course not. He was probably waiting for her to swing it open again. No doubt that was what his lady friends did. Well, she wasn't about to be one of the rank and file. She saw right through his ploy. He had wasted his time and money that night.

With determined, angry steps, Cully walked back into her bedroom, where she cast off the kimono and reached into her closet for a nightgown. As she slipped it over her smooth white body, an involuntary thought came back to her. In that one unguarded moment when he had kissed her, something had happened inside. Something had yearned to come into fruition.

Damn! she thought, grabbing up her brush and furiously brushing her hair. She didn't need this complication in her life. She didn't need any unsettling, perplexing thoughts. She had a career to set into high gear and a son to raise. That was all there was for her, and it was more than enough. Damn that man's eyes! she thought as she settled into the darkness, lying beneath the covers on her bed and bidding sleep to come. Damn him anyway!

The next day was Friday, and Cully made it a point to be in the office early. She was planning to go over her case so she would be totally refreshed on all its points when Andrea and Randolph Woolsey came into the office. The two younger heirs were a little uncomfortable about having someone so young represent their interests, even though Mr. Abernathy, the senior partner of the firm, had assured them that no one knew the case as well as, or was more qualified than, Cully. Certainly no one was as determined to win as Cully was.

Cully had been lucky to land her position with the firm as soon as she had come out of law school and passed her bar exam. Albert Abernathy had been a close friend of her father's and had watched her progress from a gangly girl to a determined young woman. He had thought that her drive would be an asset to the firm. Something about "young blood" he had told her father, who nonetheless had still not been convinced.

For the most part, Cully had done all the drudge work, learning the ropes from the bottom up, which was as it should be, she thought. She had entered the profession fully cognizant of the tedium that was often involved, had heard it all from her brothers before she had ever set foot in a law office. But there was something exhilarating and exciting about being at the heart of what made things right. She believed all the platitudes about the rights of the individual, and it was only as a concession to her parents that she had refrained from entering criminal law right away. First she'd get them used to saying, "my daughter, the lawyer," then she'd go the distance as her own kind of lawyer.

But right now she couldn't go any further until she won her case against that overbearing egotist. She stared down at the stack of papers in her portfolio, aware that Randolph Woolsey was looking rather apprehensively at her over the rim of his square-framed glasses.

"How bad does it look?" he wanted to know. "Tell us straight out. Does Serena have a case?" he asked nervously.

Cully put down the papers and sighed, leaning back in her leather-bound chair in the diminutive office that she had inherited from a previous lawyer who had gone on to bigger things within the firm. "Strictly speaking, yes," she admitted.

The answer dismayed both the man and his younger sister, who looked about as different from Serena as one could imagine. Whereas Serena was titian-haired and flamboyant—totally in keeping with Brandon Fitzhugh, Cully thought ironically—Andrea Woolsey, with her sensible clothing and bland hairdo, looked as if she were trying out for the role of a stereotypical spinster from the late 1940s. Woolsey had been disappointed in all of his children. The oldest had color but no heart. The younger ones were totally devoid of sparkle and personality. All Malcolm Woolsey had had a talent for making was money, not successful progeny, Cully thought absently.

"You make it sound hopeless," Andrea concluded unhappily. Of the two of them, she was the more businesslike. Randolph always looked uncomfortable around Cully, as if he wanted to say something but couldn't. That didn't lend itself to a very good client-lawyer relationship, but there was little Cully could do. Perhaps in time she could win them over, she thought. So far, they abided by their father's wishes and Mr. Abernathy's assurances that the firm would back Cully up in every way possible.

"I said 'strictly speaking,'" Cully repeated, a soft smile on her face. She hoped that would reassure them a little. "Your father was in the middle of setting up a living trust when he died," she reminded them. "I wish he could have hung on until it was completed."

"What good would that have done?" Andrea asked, not understanding.

"A living trust would have been very effective in keeping Serena away from the estate," Cully pointed out. "It would have been next to impossible for her to break that. But your father was a little slow in being convinced to change his mind," she said, sounding fond of the man nonetheless. Contrary and ornery though he had been, Cully missed him. She had only known him for five months, and he had been bedridden all that time, railing against the power above that had made him so, because he had been a vigorous, active man. There was something about his zest for life that had drawn Cully close, and while they sparred verbally, a deep affection had grown between them.

He was truly a man worth missing, she thought, looking sadly at his issue.

"But he left a will disinheriting her," Randolph pointed out. "You witnessed it."

Cully nodded. "Unfortunately, that isn't enough on its own," she told them. "Serena is saying that he wasn't mentally responsible, that you forced him to disinherit her by filling his head with lies about her."

"Rubbish!" Randolph muttered. Somehow the stuffy word seemed right at home on his tongue. He certainly didn't look as if he fit into the modern world, Cully thought. His smallish eyes darted about nervously as he spoke, looking as if he hoped that, despite everything, Cully could produce a magic cure right then and there and rid him and his sister of the blight that had descended upon them in the form of their older sibling.

"You have to remember that your father was a bombastic man who at times did sound as if he wasn't all there," Cully said quietly. "He was a man of vision who had no time to waste on earthbound people who couldn't see beyond their noses." She said it with admiration, thinking again what a disappointment his only son must have been to Woolsey. Randolph was such an earthbound creature. He dared not venture out in the rain without an umbrella, much less risk money on business propositions. He was perfectly content to stand pat on the fortune, sell out where it was fiscally advisable and risk nothing.

"Then what are you saying?" Andrea wanted to know. "That Serena can just waltz in and grab a share of father's money?"

"She's going to give it a good try," Cully warned.

"But I'm not saying that she's going to win. As a matter of fact, I'm going to do everything in my power to keep her from winning."

"You seem a little inexperienced," Andrea said with no preamble. While Randolph was afraid of his own shadow, Andrea was not. She meant to keep what was hers, no matter whose feelings she hurt.

Cully hadn't expected a vote of confidence from the woman. She appeared far too old-fashioned to want to go with a female lawyer, even if she was younger than Cully in years. "I assure you, I've had five years of experience fighting cases similar to yours."

"But there's going to be all that publicity, and Mr. Fitzhugh is an expert in his field," Andrea pointed out.

The mention of Brandon's name took the smile off Cully's face. "He's a magician who's given to doing sleight-of-hand tricks in court. A showman. He can't fight against a tight case, and what we're going to build, piece by piece, is a tight case. I intend to show that your father was perfectly sane when he added that codicil to the will, and after that Serena will have no course of action. She can appeal, but it won't do her any good."

"But Mr. Fitzhugh is good," Andrea argued, refusing to let the point die.

Cully had to concede that he was. "If good means being a flamboyant showman," she added.

"Good means winning," Andrea said accusingly.

"Then he's about to be proven as 'not so good,'" Cully promised. "Your father might have been gruff. He might have had unorthodox ways, but he was the sanest man I ever met, and we will prove *that* beyond a shadow of a doubt," she said.

"So what do we do?" Andrea wanted to know. She

appeared somewhat mollified by Cully's assurances. Randolph was smiling broadly at her.

"You get me a list of people your father interacted with. I want his doctor's name—"

"There were so many at the end," Randolph moaned. "He never trusted them."

"Get me all of them, then," Cully advised. "Also the names of any people he had words with, anyone he fired in the past year. Things like that."

"What possible use would that be?" Andrea asked, confused.

"The opposition is going to dig them up as ammunition," Cully told her. "I want to be prepared for any eventuality. I don't want a single surprise, is that understood?" she asked, looking from one gangly member of the family to the other.

Both nodded affirmatively.

"Good, then that'll be all for now. I'll be looking forward to hearing from you as soon as possible," Cully said, rising and ushering them out of her office.

She had no sooner shaken hands and bid them good-bye than her intercom buzzed.

"Yes, June?" she said, depressing the button.

The voice on the other end sounded both a bit dazed and a bit uncertain. "Um, there's someone to see you, Ms. Culhane."

"You're going to have to narrow it down a bit more than that, June," Cully said patiently.

"It's Brandon Fitzhugh," Cully heard a male voice —his voice—say, as he took over the intercom from her secretary.

4

Cully stared at the beige intercom on her desk in disbelief. Could that really be Brandon's voice coming out of it? she thought. The momentary silence that followed unnerved her. But not for long.

"Mr. Fitzhugh, you followed me to the Miller's-on-Kinzie restaurant—"

"A fortuitous coincidence, remember?" his smooth voice reminded her. She could almost hear him laughing at her.

"You followed me to my apartment—"

"Guilty as charged."

"And now you turn up at my office." The anger was building in her voice, despite her struggle to keep calm. "If I go to the ladies' room, are you going to turn up there, too?" she demanded.

"If you wish," came the easy reply.

"I don't wish," she snapped. "I don't wish anything

at all!" She tapped her coral-polished nails impatiently on the desk, coming down with such force that she chipped one. She glared at it, annoyed.

"Oh, I don't know about that," Brandon was saying. He sounded almost smug. "Um, do you think it's wise for us to air our dirty laundry in public this way?"

"We do not *have* any dirty laundry," she retorted, shouting at the little box. She closed her eyes. Now she was having a shouting match with him. She had never resorted to shouting to get her point across before. What was he doing to her? Was he succeeding in his campaign to unnerve her already? No, not by a long shot, she vowed to herself—but it didn't seem to help.

"Sorry," came the deep voice, almost caressing her. "A lady who dresses the way you do would be more into dry cleaning, wouldn't she?" he asked mockingly.

"Get in here!" Cully commanded.

"With pleasure," he almost purred.

Both guns. The man was going to get both guns fired at him, she swore. She could cut a person dead with a well-placed look, and she was resolved to do just that to this . . . this shyster and his dirty campaign. Her well-honed anger was to be her shield against any further efforts to get to her . . . but the shield dropped unceremoniously when Brandon entered her office.

Cully raised her blazing green eyes to the figure in her doorway and felt a wave of weakness surge through her. The memory of the previous night's kiss came back to her like a thunderclap, assaulting her senses with more force than she had originally experienced. That was the trouble with nightmares, she tried to tell herself. When they came back to haunt you, they were even more vivid.

But the warm feeling spreading through her veins at that very moment was not the kind of reaction she normally had to nightmares. The tips of her fingers tingled and her cheeks felt slightly hot, responding to the pure maleness of Brandon Fitzhugh. The sooner she got him out of her office, the better.

Cully opened her mouth to ask him sharply what his business was, but found the words blocked by Brandon's mouth assaulting hers, reviving the memory of that first kiss and adding to it. Last night had been the foundation. This morning came the structure. It built upon what was there and made it stronger, so strong that it almost frightened Cully. She had had no idea that something so overpowering existed within her. There was nothing cool and controlled about the emotions that rampaged through her, leaping up at the mere touch of his mouth and glorying in the pressure of his lips as they hypnotized her senses.

She was becoming engulfed by his kiss, rapidly losing the strength of will to do anything but enjoy it. She fought the urge to wind her arms about his neck and forced herself to try to stop his hands, which had been firmly planted on either side of her waist as the kiss started but were now inching their way upward. His palms claimed the sides of her breasts, which tingled longingly in response. With a monumental effort Cully jerked her entire body backward, freeing herself of his touch. She moved quickly to put space between them. Her eyes blazed with anger, both at him and at her own body, which had betrayed her so easily.

"Missed me?" Brandon asked, a husky lilt in his teasing voice.

Cully squared her shoulders, trying desperately to recapture the image of a controlled, competent lawyer. She sat down at her desk while Brandon, a satisfied smile on his face, walked over to the window and leaned against the sill. It appeared that he had permanently planted himself there.

"If you're not here on official business, I suggest you leave these offices," she told him crisply.

"I've come to help the counselor keep her strength up," he said, walking over to Cully slowly. The image of a panther stalking a deer flashed through Cully's mind. Well, he was going to find that she was definitely not some helpless fawn.

"What?"

"Lunch," he explained simply, still coming toward her.

Cully was getting a claustrophobic feeling. Once again there was no distance between them at all, and she was looking up into the warm sea that ebbed and flowed in his incredibly blue eyes. She didn't like looking up into his face. She wanted to get away from him, but pushing her chair back in order to stand wasn't easy. Brandon was leaning on her desk, his muscular legs barring her way.

"It's ten o'clock," she pointed out.

"Brunch, then," he compromised.

"*You* might not have any work to do, Mr. Fitzhugh, but I do," she informed him, gesturing toward her desk calendar. It was full of scribblings crammed into every conceivable corner.

Brandon turned his dark head slightly, glancing down at the calendar. "I'm impressed," he said.

"I'm not trying to impress you," Cully said defensively. The last thing in the world she wanted him to think was that she was striving for a favorable impression.

His hand came down on hers and another current of electricity shot through her. Luckily, she didn't visibly react. "That's too bad," he said. "I'm trying to impress you."

"Well, you're failing," she told him flatly, struggling to keep her physical reaction to him from surfacing. She actually liked the touch of his hand on hers. Once again, the feeling of his lips came back to her, making her long for more.

Breakfast. She had forgotten to eat breakfast, that was it, she told herself.

"Maybe I should try harder," he volunteered, his eyes scorching her.

Cully sighed. "If you truly want to impress me . . ." she said sweetly.

"Yes?"

"You'll show me how firm your grasp of the English language is and how well you can follow instructions by getting out of here. I don't appreciate this charade, and I'm not some numbskull who falls breathlessly at a man's feet for a crumb of attention," she informed him indignantly, this time managing to get up out of her seat.

The action caused her body to touch his as he straightened at the same instant. The momentary contact sent heat tingling all along her skin and brought utter distress to her soul. Why was she responding this way to someone she held in total contempt? Maybe Madge was right. Maybe she should get back into dating after all. It had been a long time since a man had held her in his arms. She was reacting out of deprivation, not because of some inherent charm on Brandon's part.

"Lady," Brandon said, smiling into her upturned face and refusing to step back and let her pass, "you've got me all wrong. I never thought of you as anything but utterly capable."

"Uh-uh. Spare me the rhetoric," she pleaded, trying to push past him. She had to get some space between them. She felt as if she needed air.

But he stood his ground. "And I'm definitely not tossing you a crumb," he said with a wicked smile, stretching out his hands. "Is this a crumb?" he asked, referring to himself.

Her icy eyes scanned his face cryptically for a moment. "That's a matter of opinion," she told him frostily.

"Lady, you've got a hard attitude," he responded, shaking his head.

"You think that's hard," she retorted, "you should try my heart." She meant for that to cut him dead.

It didn't. "I intend to," he promised.

"Sheer ice," she informed him. Somehow, her voice didn't sound quite as convincing as she had wanted it to.

"The lady doth protest too much."

"The lady is merely stating a fact."

"Facts have a way of changing," he told her. His eyes were touching her all over.

"Not the basics!" she snapped.

They were standing, their bodies tense, almost challenging one another, when the intercom buzzed.

"Saved by the bell," Brandon murmured.

"Your next appointment is here," June said after Cully depressed the intercom button.

"Tell him to wait one moment," Cully said, her eyes never leaving Brandon's face. She released the button. "You'll be going now," she said. It was a statement. She was through taking any part in the games he might have had in mind.

To her relief Brandon shrugged his shoulders. "I'll leave—for now. But my offer for lunch still stands."

"See if you can get someone else to accept it, then," she said, reseating herself and pretending to look over some papers.

He merely laughed. "End of round one, not the match," he promised her.

She looked up. "No," she agreed. "The match ends in court—with your defeat," she said firmly.

He merely smiled over his shoulder as he closed the door behind him.

She had hoped that her words would put him in his place, but it was obvious to her that they hadn't.

Cully went to lunch, peeking into the office building's lobby first. She was afraid that at any moment Brandon would pop out of some corner and grab her arm, dragging her off to his car. But he didn't show up, much to her relief. And, perhaps, just a little to her disappointment.

Overwork, she told herself as she lunched on a chef's salad. She was suffering from fatigue and overwork. That was what came of trying to be a career woman and supermom at the same time, she thought, picking up a leaf of slightly wilted lettuce and toying with it. Her appetite, normally quite healthy, was mysteriously gone. There had been articles in all the leading magazines expounding on the demise of supermom, but she had never believed that they referred to her. She was special, she had told herself, and could manage both parts of her life very well—all by herself.

So why did her mind keep drifting back to the way Brandon had looked in her office, his thick, straight black hair just kissing the back of his collar, making him look like a Brooks Brothers model instead of a lawyer? He looked more like a TV version of a lawyer than the real thing. That was why he got by on dramatics, she thought, hunting out the strips of ham in the bowl. There were five. The owners were cutting back, she thought sadly, retiring her fork and taking a sip of her diet soda. Her stomach was neither satisfied nor empty, just strangely unsettled.

Enough of Brandon Fitzhugh and his theatrics, she told herself. She rose to pay her check and then walked the block and a half back to her office. People scurried about all around her, and yet she suddenly felt so lonely. She had never realized how dull and cold everything about this city looked. Everything seemed colored in various shades of gray. What was wrong with her? She loved Chicago. Brandon must be doing this to her. She walked back briskly, trying to purge him from her thoughts.

The subject of Brandon was forced back into her mind when she walked into her oak paneled office. Standing on her desk, in direct contrast to the stately black leather bound lawbooks stacked neatly to one side, were a dozen long-stemmed roses. They were arranged in a cut glass vase she had long forgotten about.

"June?" Cully called, not closing the door behind her as she stared at the flowers.

June, a tall, storklike woman with glasses that resided permanently on the tip of her nose, came in. "I took the liberty of taking them out of the box," she explained, nodding toward the roses. "I didn't know when you were coming back from lunch with him."

"I didn't go to lunch with him," Cully informed her tersely. This had to stop. People might start thinking that Brandon was influencing her.

"Oh," June remarked, surprised. "Well, anyway, the box is there—with a card," she said, pointing to the leather sofa, then marching back to her desk. June, Cully noted, marched everywhere, even to the water cooler. Must come from having a father in the military, she thought absently as she fingered the shell-colored envelope in her hand. Who would want to send her roses? she wondered. It wasn't her birthday, and she hadn't won a case in court for several weeks. Who . . . ?

The strong masculine hand stared back at her. Brandon! She tossed the card down on her desk, then picked it up again. "I only want to be friends with a lovely lady," the words read.

"Right, so you can skin her alive in court," she muttered. "Well, no way, Mr. Fitzhugh. This is one lady who isn't falling for it," she said to the card.

Now she was talking to cards. Cully closed her eyes, wishing she'd had a strong drink at lunch instead of a diet soda.

She heard June sigh and turned around. The

woman was peeking into her office. "Wish someone would send me roses," June murmured.

Cully picked up the vase and thrust it into the taller woman's hands. "Here, consider them sent," she said cripsly.

June opened her owl eyes wide behind her wire-rimmed spectacles. "But they're yours," she protested.

"Right. To do with as I wish. I wish to give them to you, so take them out of here," Cully said, waving them and June out the door. "I have work to do," she added, taking off her jacket and flinging it over the back of her leather chair.

June walked out, a "thank you" and a sneeze punctuating the air. June had hay fever, Cully remembered as the door closed.

But the door hadn't closed on the subject of roses. They began arriving twice daily, once in the morning, once after lunch. All bore similar messages that politely invited Cully out to either lunch or dinner. That went on for a week, and Cully ran out of secretaries in the firm to give her roses to. Brandon was definitely getting on her nerves.

The straw that broke the camel's back came the afternoon she returned from lunch to find not one, not two, but five dozen roses, still cradled in their silver-toned boxes, neatly arranged on her desk and peering out of green tissue paper. Cully's door was open and as she walked in she could feel the stares of all the secretaries and her coworkers as they waited to see her reaction.

One of the lawyers winked at her knowingly, which only added fuel to her inner fire. "Unless you have a nervous tick, Rutherford," she said to the round man who smirked at her, "I suggest you save that wink for where it belongs."

"Why, Cully, this is a side of you we've never seen before," someone else chuckled, his arms folded across his vest.

"Actually," she said flippantly, "I'm taking a home correspondence course on how to become financially independent as a florist," she quipped. She took a deep breath. "June, get these out of here."

"What'll I do with them?" June asked, staring at the red splendor that lay about Cully's desk like a deep velvet carpet.

"Send them to the cemetery in preparation for Mr. Fitzhugh's arrival," Cully said. "Okay, show's over," she informed the crowd, closing her door on them. She walked over and reached for her phone. She was going to put an end to this once and for all, she thought, pulling out a card from one of the boxes. She dialed the florist's number.

But the call yielded no satisfaction. The sweet-voiced lady on the other end of the line could not be persuaded to stop the orders of roses from coming. The customer paid, the customer got delivery. And did Cully appreciate the cost of roses these days? Perhaps she and the young man could patch things up, the woman suggested genially.

Cully stared at the beige phone in her hand as if it had a life of its own. For some reason she found herself trying to reason with the woman, telling her that there was nothing to "patch up."

"Oh, that's not what he told me," the lady chuckled. "Been rather hard on him, haven't you?" she suggested kindly.

Cully stopped the woman before she got any further, saying yes, yes, she'd call him right away. Then she hung up, annoyed. Well, there was nothing left to do but call Brandon.

The thought immediately sent a strange, prickling sensation rushing through her body. Great! She was probably allergic to the very thought of him and would break out any minute, she muttered to herself. Brandon's number was written on every card he had sent her, so she was spared the humiliation of having to ask June to look it up for her. She couldn't bear any more knowing glances.

At that moment Albert Abernathy entered the room. She glanced up and saw the smile on his lips. He was obviously amused and bemused at the same time. Cully looked at the white-haired senior partner of the firm and waited. Slowly she retracted her hand from the phone.

"I hear you've been the recipient of flowers, Eve," he said, making himself comfortable in the crisp, soft brown leather armchair that was closest to Cully. His brown eyes studied her closely, but the act didn't make her ill at ease. Abernathy was the personification of a nineteenth-century statesman, Cully thought. That was probably why he got on so well with juries.

"Not flowers," Cully said with a touch of annoyed despair in her voice. "A whole garden."

An amused chuckle rumbled out of the distinguished man's chest. "From Brandon Fitzhugh," he added quietly. Cully nodded, waiting to see his reaction. "Trying to bribe you, I see," Abernathy said, as if it were the most common thing in the world.

Cully shrugged. "That's what I think."

"Is it working?" he asked, arching one snowy brow

in her direction. He seemed to know the answer to his question ahead of time.

At least Cully hoped he did. "Not by a long shot," she said firmly. "I was just about to call him and tell him to stop wasting his money and my time."

"That's my girl," the man said with the conviction of an old family friend. He rose from the chair. "But I'd be careful if I were you, Eve. The man's sharp."

"So am I," Cully said, a twinkle coming into her eye.

"I wouldn't have you working here if you weren't," Abernathy informed her, his voice serious. "Still," he hesitated at the door, "Fitzhugh is a handsome devil . . ." Once again he appeared to be studying Cully.

"I hadn't noticed," she said a bit too quickly.

"Oh-oh," Abernathy said, shaking his head. Cully raised her eyes toward him quizzically. He didn't elaborate on his comment, but she caught his meaning immediately and tried not to flush. Of course Brandon was handsome. Anyone could see that. Why had she denied it so vehemently? *The lady doth protest too much.* Brandon's words came floating back to her.

Abernathy paused, his hand on the doorknob. "Eve, I won't presume to tell you how to run your personal life. I've always encouraged you to enjoy yourself. You work much too hard," he observed, glancing about at the different briefs that lined her table against the bay window, "and as long as the Woolsey case doesn't enter into your conversation, there's nothing unethical about having a relationship with the man."

Cully opened her mouth in protest, but Abernathy

went on as if he hadn't seen her attempt to deny his statement.

"But he *is* an operator. While I *am* sure that he will not undermine your determination to win the case, I fear that getting emotionally entangled with him might be disastrous to you. He has a merited reputation, you know."

"Yes, I know," Cully replied firmly.

Abernathy nodded. "Just as long as you know," he said softly, then left the room.

Well, at least he had confidence in her as a lawyer, Cully thought, still looking at the closed door as she reached for the phone. But it bothered her that Abernathy thought of her as such a pushover as a woman. She was just as strong a woman as she was a lawyer. Hadn't she proved that when she had picked up the pieces of her life after her husband had walked out on her? Did everyone think that just because Brandon Fitzhugh had a wonderfully charming, crooked smile and eyes so blue they rivaled the sky on a crisp autumn day that she was going to be putty in his hands? She wouldn't have been, even if he had just been pursuing her out of some sort of physical attraction. Knowing that he was only out to dull her wits when they met in court merely added to her determination not to succumb to him.

With renewed single-mindedness, Cully punched the buttons on her telephone.

It took her a while to clear her way through a network of operators and receptionists, all of whom seemed zealously to want to protect the man from any unwanted calls. Undoubtedly they were used to getting calls from Brandon's former flames, she thought.

But when she gave her name, obstacles magically disappeared and there she was, on each higher plateau. Finally she reached him.

"Fitzhugh," came the rumbling voice.

It unnerved her just a touch. "Ah, the man himself," she said with a hint of sarcasm in her voice. "I think I could have gotten through to the President with less trouble."

"Eve," he said, his voice sounding delighted. She could almost see him coming to attention. Why did he want to win this case so badly? she wondered. What had Serena promised him in exchange for victory?

Despite everything, Cully felt almost as if he were petting her, his voice caressing the single syllable of her name. He made it sound almost like a romantic pronouncement.

"I'm flattered you went through all that trouble for me."

"Well, don't be," she said crisply. "I'm calling about the flowers."

"So they've arrived," he said, his voice pleased. What was he wearing? Abruptly her mind recoiled in horror. Why was she fantasizing about what he was wearing? What *was* the matter with her?

"Arrived? The landing on the beach on D-day attracted less attention. I want you to stop flowering me to death," she insisted.

"Well, only you can arrange that."

"How?" she asked wearily.

"Have dinner with me," he replied smoothly.

"Said the spider to the fly," she quipped.

"Why, Ms. Culhane, are you impugning my honor?" he asked with overdone tones of alarm. "Or is it that you don't trust yourself?" he asked, his voice lower, sending waves of uninvited heat rippling through her.

"If I don't trust myself about anything, it has to do with keeping myself from strangling you."

"That impulse will pass," he guaranteed.

"I doubt it," she said cryptically.

"As you wish," he answered obligingly. "Anything to have your hands on me."

Cully's hand tightened on the receiver. "You've got to stop sending me roses. People are beginning to have the wrong idea about us."

"So am I."

"I'm not interested in your ideas, Mr. Fitzhugh!"

"So," he went on, unruffled, "how about dinner?"

"Don't you hear me?" she cried. "I don't want to eat with you."

"Then watch me eat."

"No!"

"I was thinking of sending wreaths next, seeing as how you're burying my heart . . ."

"All right!" she cried in exasperation. "If I agree to one meal, will you stop sending me flowers?" she demanded.

"I promise. Tonight?"

She closed her eyes. Her inner voice murmured, *You'll be sorry.*

"Tonight," she agreed.

"Seven?"

"Fine." It wasn't, but what else could she do? "Good-bye," she said before he could say anything further.

She dropped the receiver on the cradle with a muted bang, and it fell off. Even her aim was going.

5

"You're going out with him?" Timmy asked excitedly, shifting from one foot to another as he stood in Cully's bedroom, watching her put her makeup on.

Cully glanced at her son. She hadn't seen him so animated in a long time. Why did it have to be Brandon Fitzhugh who brought such color to his cheeks? Why did it have to be Brandon who brought such color to her own cheeks? she wondered as she held her blusher brush suspended in midair. Looking at herself in the mirror, she saw that she really didn't need any artificial color. Her cheeks looked rosy, glowing even. That's anger, her common sense whispered, rationalizing.

"It's either go out with him or be buried alive in roses," she told the boy. She tried to make him understand. "I'm only going out with him under duress," she said, putting down her eye shadow wand after she had succeeded in highlighting her emerald eyes just enough to make them a shade away from bewitching. Cully ushered Timmy back into the living room. "I've really got to get you enrolled in that big brother program," she said as the boy plopped down on the sofa. That way, she added mentally, he wouldn't be so susceptible to the likes of Brandon Fitzhugh.

But Timmy shook his head glumly. "That's okay, Mom. I don't want some stranger talking down to me. Elliot's got one," he said, referring to his best friend, "and he says it's a drag."

"We'll see," Cully said nonetheless. The boy needed something to get his mind off matchmaking. He had been trying to couple her with Brandon with almost every breath he took. Brandon was all Timmy had talked about since the man had waylaid them in the restaurant. She had to put an end to it somehow. It was bad enough that the insufferable man was carrying on his own campaign of nerves against her. She didn't want her son aiding and abetting him.

Just then the doorbell rang.

"It's him!" Timmy announced, bolting to life as he made it to the door in an incredibly short time.

Before Cully could reach him, Timmy was undoing the locks and pulling the door open. She could see her son beaming as he looked up.

"Hi, Tiger," Brandon said to him. "Mind if I come in?"

"He might not, but I do," Cully muttered as Brandon stepped inside.

His sharp blue eyes washed over Cully's form, showing his deep appreciation. His sensuous lips widened in a smile. "Lovelier each time," he said, extending a long silver box toward her. "For you," he added needlessly, his eyes never leaving her face.

Cully glanced down at the box, relieved that she had something else to look at instead of those deep pools that unnerved her so.

"I'm surprised that there are any roses left in the city," she said, opening the box.

"There aren't. These were flown in from the next state—just for you," he said, taking the box back from her, his fingers purposely brushing against hers teasingly. He seemed to watch for the hoped-for effect, which she struggled not to show. Why did she have to react this way to him? Why wasn't her will strong enough for her to block out his sultry vibrations? She hated him, so why was part of her betraying her?

"Are we going to play tug-of-war with the box?" she wanted to know.

"No, I was just going to hand this to Tim so that he could put them in water." He turned toward Timmy. "Someone staying with you until we get back, Tiger?" he asked, giving the box to Timmy.

His question surprised Cully. His concern appeared genuine. Could he actually like children? she wondered.

"Madge is staying with him," Cully said. "That is, if she gets here." Cully glanced at her watch. "Maybe she can't make it," she mused out loud, suddenly hopeful. It wasn't like Madge to be late. "We'll have to cancel dinner if that's the case." Oh, please, let that be the case, she thought.

"Fine by me," Brandon said, walking over to the sofa and making himself comfortable. "We can send out and have dinner here."

This wasn't working the way she wanted it to. Cully pressed her lips together. She became nervous, recalling the way the evening had ended the last time he had "stayed for dinner." Just then the doorbell rang again. She sighed with relief.

Brandon rose to answer the door, completely taking over. "Don't look so relieved," he whispered as he passed her. His breath tickled her neck. "I wasn't planning on seducing you with your son watching."

Oh, she hated his smugness. Her eyes narrowed. "I detest violence, Mr. Fitzhugh," she warned, "but I'm quite good at it."

Brandon stopped, his hand on the doorknob. "Tell me more," he murmured against her smoothly combed hair. "You're getting me excited."

Cully elbowed him out of the way, determined to answer her own door. She shot him a murderous look as she swung it open. Madge stepped in, smiling at Brandon before she even looked at Cully. Another vote for his side, Cully thought.

When Madge did turn her eyes toward her niece, a look of total satisfaction was evident in them. "You didn't tell me you were going out with Brandon," she said.

Brandon slipped his arm around Cully's shoulders. "It probably slipped her mind in her excitement," he assured the older woman.

Cully shrugged off his arm, hating the unbidden tingle that cascaded from her shoulders down to her breasts. To her horror, she felt her nipples tightening and forming visible shapes beneath her turquoise knit dress. One hasty glance toward Brandon told her that he was quite aware of her reaction—and proud of it.

"Well, let's get this thing over with," Cully said, grabbing her purse.

"You make it sound as if you're taking a dose of castor oil," Madge chided, walking them to the door. Timmy wasn't far behind, dogging Brandon's shadow.

"No," Cully said firmly. "Castor oil is supposed to be healthy for you," she said dryly, walking out past Brandon as he threw open the door for her.

"And not habit forming," Brandon added.

Cully whirled about on her heel. "Neither are you," she retorted, catching his meaning.

"Don't count on it, Evie," he told her with a meaningful laugh, winking at Madge and Timmy.

Cully felt her blood boiling. He was using everything against her. One look at her family told her that they were charmed down to their very toes.

"You should live so long," she heard herself saying. Now there was a snappy comeback, her legal mind taunted her.

"I intend to," he said, taking her elbow as they went to the elevator.

"You really fight dirty, you know?" Cully said sharply.

The elevator arrived and they walked in. Brandon reached across her to press the button for the ground floor, somehow managing to brush against her breasts as he did so. Cully pulled back, glaring.

"I fight to win," he replied, not denying her accusation.

At least he was decent enough to be honest about what he was up to, Cully thought, disliking the way his eyes roamed over her as they rode down in silence. Decent? The man didn't know the meaning of the word. Probably didn't even know how to spell it.

Once outside, Brandon hailed a cab, and soon Cully found herself being helped into the back seat of a taxicab.

"I thought you had your own car," she said, attempting to slide over and leave a little space between them. It failed. Sliding wasn't all that easy on the cracked upholstery, and even when she did manage to do so, Brandon just followed her, getting in closer.

"I do," he answered mildly. "But it has bucket seats."

That was rather a strange excuse. "So?" she heard herself asking.

"So I couldn't be doing this if we were separated by bucket seats," he told her, slipping his arm around her shoulders, his fingers curling about her arm.

"I have news for you. You can't do this anyway," she said, leaning forward and undraping his arm.

Brandon merely laughed and let her go. Cully sat up straight, keeping her eyes ahead and fervently wishing that this so-called date was over with. She didn't know just how much of this man she could take without losing her temper completely.

Was that the real reason? a little voice whispered.

Cully hated little voices. They never said what you wanted them to.

"A penny for your thoughts," Brandon said after allowing the silence to go on for a few minutes.

She turned her face toward him, hoping she looked sufficiently annoyed. "I'm contemplating murder," she told him coldly.

"They'd never let you get away with it," he said, amused.

"Oh, I don't know. They'd probably give me a medal for rendering a service to society."

"Am I as bad as all that?" he asked, his strong hand taking hers. Despite her struggle, he uncurled her clenched hand and wrapped her fingers about his. She could feel the heat from his body warming her, making her very uncomfortable. She rolled open a window, hoping the night air and the cold breeze would awaken her drugged senses before it was too late.

"You're worse," she said, her voice not nearly as forceful as she would have liked. He was unraveling something inside, sidling up to her that closely. His body was crowding her, touching her, making her yearn for things she had no business wanting from him.

Brandon didn't answer her accusation. Oh no, he was going to kiss her again, she thought desperately as she saw him bend his head. Her eyes darted toward the rearview mirror. But the cab driver's eyes were where they should be, on the road.

And then it was too late. She was being engulfed, her senses assaulted as Brandon's strong, gentle fingers played over her neck, stroking it lightly as he pressed his lips to hers.

Why wasn't she pulling back, hitting him, biting his lip, something? Why was she letting herself be affected in this manner? Her mind was reeling almost drunkenly in response to the feel of his lips crushing hers. She hated him, yet there she was, going out with him. He was on the lower rung of humanity as far as she was concerned, yet when he kissed her, she responded with a flame that had never had a part in her life before. What was there about the man that turned her into such a mass of contradictions?

His hand slid from her throat down her shoulder, pulling her closer to him and seeming to burn away the layers of clothing that served as her protective barrier. He melted away the cab driver, the cab, the entire city. For a timeless moment nothing existed or was real to Cully except for the feel of Brandon's caressing hands and the startling need that was forming within her.

"We're here." The cab driver's harsh voice broke into the swirling heat just in time.

Cully roused herself, or tried to. "Where?" Was that her voice sounding so breathless?

"The restaurant," Brandon said. She thought she detected a chuckle in his voice. The thought caused her to pull back and square her shoulders. Her dress was slightly askew and she adjusted it, embarrassed, her cheeks blazing.

Brandon fished out a twenty from his pocket and handed it to the driver as Cully looked on.

"Your change," the driver called after them as Brandon began ushering Cully toward the door of the Azuma Sukiyaki restaurant.

"Keep it," Brandon said brightly.

"Rather free with your money, aren't you?" Cully commented as the cab pulled away from the curb.

Brandon put a guiding hand on her shoulder. The action was an intimate one in a strange sort of way, as if his hand belonged there. Cully's normal impulse to shrug it away was curtailed by a warm, almost protected feeling that was subtly spreading to all corners of her body.

"It's a grueling, thankless job," he said, nodding his head in the direction of the departing cab. "Maybe that'll make up for the guy who doesn't give him anything."

"Noble thought," she said, but for once there was no edge to her voice.

Brandon smiled down at her as they came to the entrance. "I told you, I'm rather a noble person once you get to know me."

Cully said nothing. Instead she reached up to wipe away the telltale traces of her pink lipstick from Brandon's generous mouth. As her thumb glossed over his lips, Brandon kissed it. She felt the fleeting movement of his tongue against her flesh and a sultry sensation sprang up, immediately gliding up her arm and through her body.

"Destroying the evidence?" he asked her humorously.

"Exactly," she said, trying not to show him the effect that he had had on her.

"While you're destroying evidence, what are you going to do about my pounding heart?" he asked, taking her hand from his mouth and putting it over his chest.

"Ignore it," she replied, taking her hand back.

He laughed softly. The sound was deep and rich. "You're a hard lady, Evie."

But it wasn't meant as a criticism, she thought, as she entered the restaurant one step ahead of him.

The interior of the Japanese restaurant had an immediate effect on Cully, and she wondered if Brandon had planned it that way. The atmosphere was tranquil and seemed to radiate a deep peacefulness. The hurried pace of Chicago life outside the walls seemed to melt away in the face of the soothing aura of the dimly lit establishment. As Cully's looked about herself slowly, she saw that the blanket of darkness was gently parted here and there by colorful art works. Intricately detailed vases and statues of gods forgotten by all except the authors of dusty books containing legends and folktales caught her eye.

For a moment it almost seemed as if there was no one in attendance. The only noise that Cully heard was the gentle rippling sound of water as it spilled over a wall and then flowed into a fish pond that was to the far right of the cashier's area.

Then, from out of the shadows, came a slender figure, her body neatly cloaked in a ceremonial kimono.

"Welcome," she greeted them, a soft smile on her young face. She turned to lead the way to a little room with lovely paper walls depicting a sunrise in a quaint Japanese village. The hostess stopped at the entrance of the room, politely expectant. Cully removed her shoes, as did Brandon. But while removing his shoes made no discernible difference in Brandon's height, the loss of hers left Cully quite a bit shorter. She felt exceedingly vulnerable as she looked up at his towering frame.

Brandon gestured her toward a yellow pillow bordering one side of a low black table. "Makes it a little difficult to slide out your chair for you," he told her drolly.

"I can manage," she assured him, folding her slender legs to the side as she seated herself.

"Would you care for anything to drink?" the hostess

asked in lilting tones. Her voice fit the atmosphere. Cully nodded, but before she could open her mouth, she heard Brandon order for her.

"The lady would like a Singapore Sling," he said, looking at Cully. "Did I get that right?" he asked. It was a rhetorical question; he knew he had.

"Been doing more homework?" she asked, wondering if all her vital statistics sat somewhere embedded in a home computer that Brandon flashed on in the morning to aid him in his crusade to unnerve her.

"I like to know things about the lady I'm squiring," he murmured softly.

It was almost a purr, and it sent another wave of electricity through her. He was good, she'd grant him that. He could produce these reactions at will without the benefit of even touching her, Cully thought in grudging admiration. Oh, he was a worthy opponent. But he mustn't win . . . at least not in court, a tiny voice added.

Cully lowered her eyes from his as she looked at her menu. She heard him order a Scotch and soda while she ran her nail down the long list of tempting dishes. She hadn't realized how hungry she was. Seafood was her favorite, and there was a variety to choose from. The hostess waited discreetly until Cully had made up her mind to have the shrimp tempura.

Brandon's order came quickly on the heels of her own. A swish of the hostess's kimono and the woman was gone, leaving Cully alone with Brandon in a room that seemed to be growing smaller.

It had become almost overbearingly small by the time Cully was given her frosty drink. She wondered why they didn't at least hear the soft, droning murmur of other voices coming from the adjoining rooms. After all, the walls were only paper. The feeling of isolation made her nervous. Absently she twirled the tiny umbrella that had decorated her drink.

Brandon's deep blue eyes watched her, making her aware of what she was doing. She put down the umbrella and took another deep sip of her drink. The luscious fruit concoction slid easily down her throat. She saw Brandon's smile deepen. That was a mistake, her natural warning system told her. Liquor was not going to help her at a time like this. Rather, it would ally itself with him.

"Thank you for going out with me," Brandon said.

She raised her eyebrows. He was being too nice. "I had very little choice," she reminded him. "It was either that or watch while every rosebush in the country was stripped," she said. She lowered her eyes. Brandon's smile was permeating every pore of her body. "I didn't want that on my conscience."

"I didn't know you were ecology minded," he said, his voice teasing her.

"I believe everything should be given a chance to survive and keep its rightful place in the sun," she told him quite seriously as the hostess returned, bearing their food. The woman was gone the next moment, having done her job faultlessly. Cully hardly took any notice of her. She was watching the strange smile playing on Brandon's lips.

"Too bad my father wasn't more like you."

What an odd thing to say, she thought. She had to know what he meant by that. She told herself that it was a good tactic to get to know her opponent thoroughly, but her curiosity went deeper than that.

"What do you mean?" she asked, setting her drink down—heavens, was it almost gone so soon? She picked up her chopsticks in order to tackle the meal.

"He was a doctor. Best doctor around, actually," Brandon admitted with a real respect. "He wanted me to become the second best doctor around. Apprentice myself to him, as it were, and step into his shoes once he felt ready to retire. He never forgave me for ruining his plans," Brandon told her, deftly working his own chopsticks.

He was faring a lot better than she was, Cully thought in self-disparagement. Managing chopsticks was something that she had somehow never mastered, despite her normal gracefulness. Cully glanced up at Brandon after another futile attempt on her part to gather up some rice.

"Was becoming a lawyer that important to you?" she asked as a shrimp fell from her chopsticks. Doggedly, she went after it again.

"The most important thing in the world," he answered. "Important enough for me to get myself cut out of his will and his favor," he concluded.

Cully was surprised. She hadn't thought that there was anything Brandon cared about to that extent. Perhaps he wasn't as shallow as she thought. A pang came to her as she remembered her own father's face when she had announced that she was going to become a lawyer.

"A lot of fathers have preconceived notions as to what they want their offspring to be. Mine was adamant about having his become lawyers—his male children," she added pointedly. A rueful smile came to her lips. "When I told him I wanted to do the same, he went through the roof, striking down all the reasons he had cited to my brothers when he had been talking them into taking up the law."

"He was a chauvinist," Brandon said, filling in her thoughts.

Cully nodded. "Yes."

"Like me," he added humorously.

The smile was infectious. "Yes," she said again. Then she looked at him seriously. A small feeling of kinship had been born of their mutual struggle to set foot on the same path. "Look, Mr. Fitzhugh—"

"Brandon," he reminded her.

"Brandon," she conceded. "I know very well why you asked me out, why you almost buried me in red roses, and why you're haunting my every waking moment."

"Am I haunting your every waking moment?" he asked, leaning forward. His eyes almost hypnotized her.

That had been an unwise choice of words. She licked her lips, looking for a way out. But he provided it for her; he didn't keep her on the spot. At the same time, he also didn't let her finish her statement.

"Here, let me," he said, suddenly moving closer to her. He got behind her and took her hand, forcing her fingers into the correct position for the chopsticks. "You'll find you have less trouble this way," he instructed, encouraging her to pick up several grains of rice under his watchful eye. For some reason, when she did as he bid, it worked.

"There," he said triumphantly. "Now you do that as gracefully as you do everything else."

Still he made no move to return to his own pillow.

Instead, he lowered his head slightly and softly kissed the side of her neck. She knew she should have left her hair down!

Instantly a warm charge coursed through her veins, ignited by the softness of his kiss. His hands were no longer near the chopsticks, but on her shoulders. His chest was against her back, the hard, muscular impression it made transmitting itself to her consciousness. She ought to pull away, she told herself. No, she'd wait just a moment longer. Her heart pounded; her senses were wildly alert, craving another dose of excitement on which to thrive.

This had to stop, she thought with the closest thing to panic she had experienced in a long time. She turned her head to say so, but the words never got past her lips. Her lips became occupied in something far more compelling as Brandon's mouth covered hers.

His hand slid down to the front of Cully's dress, at first exploring the soft skin there, then ever so slowly opening the first button and then the next and the next. His fingers lovingly caressed what he discovered beneath the lacy bra.

"I won't . . . be . . . played with . . . like a . . . pawn," she said, but the note of accusation in her voice died before it ever came to fruition.

"I don't intend to play with you like a pawn, Evie," Brandon breathed between the sharp, butterfly assaults his lips made on her throat and the upper planes of her breasts. How had he gotten around her like that? her mind demanded feebly. "If I play you at all, it will be like a finely tuned instrument—like a Stradivarius."

His arms went about her in an almost fierce grip and he held her close to him. She was cradled against his chest as his hot mouth devoured hers.

Then, behind them, the silk screen door opened and the melodious voice of the hostess asked if everything was all right.

6

Cully sprang away from Brandon, keeping her back to the hostess. What had come over her? her mind demanded. She was necking in a public place. Necking? It had gone past that.

But the hostess discreetly pretended to take no notice as she withdrew once more, having been assured by Brandon that everything was just fine. Easily, he slid back onto his pillow.

"I'm sorry if that embarrassed you," he said kindly.

Cully fought hard to keep the blush from her face as she quickly rebuttoned her dress. She saw him staring. "You're very good with buttons," she muttered. She hoped he didn't see how flustered she really was.

"If inspired the right way," he said lightly. "And you would inspire a dead man to plead for just one more chance at life," he told her, whispering the words ever so softly.

Cully took a deep breath. "At least I learned the proper way to manage chopsticks," she said. And a little more about myself, she added silently.

"Always glad to help," Brandon told her. "—With anything." The words were so pregnant with meaning that Cully didn't want to explore them.

But explore them she did, over and over again during the rest of the evening, which went far better than she had expected. Brandon became the embodiment of a perfect gentleman. By the end of the evening Cully found herself talking to him without the wary note in her voice. She discovered that she actually enjoyed conversing with him. The evening melted away into charming small talk.

Brandon left her at her door without even trying to press the clear advantage he had gained, but the one brief kiss he planted so ardently upon her lips burned a deep impression into her consciousness.

Cully watched him go, shaking her head, confused as to what to think. Brandon had shown her how very vulnerable she was, how easily, despite all her mental girdings, she could succumb to the flaming pressure of his lips. And yet he had made no further attempts to seduce her. Could it be that she was actually wrong about his motives after all?

But her suspicions died hard. Perhaps, she thought as she let herself into her apartment, it had been the effect of the alcohol she had had. It had fogged her thinking. Or maybe she felt the way she did because she hadn't gone out with men nearly enough since her divorce. After all, Abernathy had warned her that Brandon was very, very good. She could easily be lulled into a false sense of security and led into a tender trap.

"How did it go?" Madge asked, almost pouncing on Cully as she walked in.

Cully smiled. Poor Madge. "Don't start sending out wedding invitations just yet," she told her with a fond smile.

She fielded all of Madge's eager questions until the woman finally tired of trying to pin her down. "Well," Madge finally said with a sigh as she picked up her novel from the coffee table and tucked it under her arm, "It's a start, anyway."

Yes, it was that, Cully mused after she had locked the door. But what exactly was it the start of? A beautiful friendship? A romance? Or a lost court case? Cully, normally so confident, was no longer very sure of anything.

"I thought I should get back to you as soon as possible," Randolph Woolsey was saying to Cully the next day. His Adam's apple danced up and down nervously as he uttered the words, and Cully wondered if he had something else on his mind besides the stack of papers he was handing her.

She arranged the papers meticulously in neat piles. "You've done very well," she said, smiling. "I'm sure this will help me a great deal."

Randolph raised his long body as he tried to point out several different facts for her. "The bottom list contains the names of people I thought might be hostile toward my father."

Cully looked at the page he was pointing to. It was quite a list. "You think there might be this many people?" she asked, scanning the names and wondering how long it would take to get in contact with each of them.

"He wasn't an easy man to get along with," Randolph said. His voice was rather woebegone. His thin shoulders shrugged in answer to her question, causing the dull green suit to shift on its own. Brandon's clothes moved with him. Now why was she thinking of Brandon at a time like this?

Ever since the previous night, fleeting thoughts of Brandon had been sneaking up on her no matter how hard she tried to shut them out of her mind. In the light of day, Cully had almost convinced herself that while the night had been lovely, it had happened, in part, because she had missed male companionship. She was a normal, healthy female, and Brandon had been at the right place at the wrong time. That was why she had responded the way she had. She had to get out more.

She looked up from the pages, wondering if Randolph could see that she was just pretending to read through them and that her mind was somewhere else. You're cheating your client, her mind nagged. She realized that he was looking at her rather nervously.

"Is there something you want to say?" she asked, her voice almost coaxing him.

Randolph rose from his chair, clasping his long, bony fingers behind his back. He wandered over to her window. Cully waited patiently until he turned around again, pursing his wafer-thin lips together in an attempt to form the first words. Nothing happened. He swallowed. Then, drawing a breath, he finally said, "You see, there's this fund raiser . . ."

"Yes?" she asked encouragingly, not exactly sure what he was getting at.

The bright Chicago sun streamed in through her large window, highlighting the growing redness of

Randolph's face. "I was wondering, perhaps, um, if you had nothing better to do and it didn't interfere with the case, that maybe you could . . . ?" His voice trailed off as he looked almost pathetically in her direction.

How could someone like this be Woolsey's son? she wondered, trying to keep the thought from showing on her face. How unlike Brandon he was. Now that was stupid, she chided herself. Brandon was a theatrical type, given to dramatics. Of course he'd be able to ask a woman out with flair—or hound her to death until she went out with him. Randolph's invitation was . . . refreshing, she told herself, knowing full well that she was stretching the word to its limit.

"I'd love to." She smiled, remembering her promise to herself to begin dating more. Might as well start here. Besides, it might put him more at ease with her, which would be good for their client-lawyer relations. "What time?" she wanted to know.

Randolph looked stunned at his good fortune. He smiled, beaming at her with a row of slightly misaligned teeth. "Tomorrow."

"Could you narrow that down just a little more?" Cully asked, trying to hide a smile.

"I'm sorry. I'm a little awkward," he confessed.

"I hadn't noticed," Cully lied charitably.

"I'll pick you up at seven, if that's all right with you."

"That's fine with me," she assured him.

Cully tried to tell herself that a woman didn't have to look forward with bated breath to every date she had. Besides, she *had* been a recluse because of her ex-husband, and it was time she did something about it.

Still, she had to admit that when she had been getting ready for her date with Brandon, there had been a definite feeling of excitement radiating through her, despite her protests. Getting ready to go out with Randolph was . . . well, kind of like studying the brief for a cut and dried court case. It did very little to fire her imagination.

Timmy had been excited enough for both of them until he had learned that it wasn't Brandon who was escorting his mother, but someone named Randolph.

"Does Brandon know?" he asked accusingly, staring at her as she put on her makeup.

"Brandon doesn't have to know," she said to his reflection in her mirror. She ran a comb casually through her hair. "Timmy, when I get back, you and I are going to have a long talk about Brandon," she told him.

Her model son was looking at her with sullen, accusing eyes, as if she were betraying him. He was too young to be going through the awkward age, she told herself, hurrying to put the finishing touches on her toilette. Her brows knitted together slightly. Even when Brandon wasn't there, he invaded every nook and cranny of her life and home.

Timmy's expression didn't get any better when he saw Randolph. And Cully had to admit that Randolph did not cut a very impressive figure. Compared to the flamboyant Brandon Fitzhugh, he fell miles short. She quickly ushered the man out and away from the scrutinizing gazes of her aunt and son.

Conversation did not flow easily on the way to the

posh residence of the woman holding the fundraiser, a Mrs. Agatha McBain. The event, Cully found out, was being held on behalf of some almost extinct species of bird.

"She's an old family friend," Randolph told Cully, sitting a proper distance away from Cully in the chauffeured limousine. "She's been crazy about birds ever since I've known her. She's spending quite a lot on this party," he added in hushed, confidential tones.

This promised to be some experience, Cully thought, looking out the window at the passing traffic.

There were a lot of jewel-studded people already there by the time Cully and Randolph arrived. Cully cast her eye about the gaily decorated ballroom as a starched and pressed butler took her fur stole. Most of these people, she thought, could easily be transplanted to some embassy function. She was surprised to see that there were so many bird fanciers in Chicago. And . . . Cully's eyes grew wide as she zeroed in on an imposing figure standing in a far corner of the room. Brandon! There was a lustrous redhead draped on his arm.

His startling blue eyes, brilliant even at a distance, looked in her direction at that moment. He appeared as surprised to see her as she had been to see him, but his easy composure immediately slid into place as he nodded toward her in greeting. Cully nodded back, telling herself not to stare. But it wasn't Brandon she was actually staring at. It was the woman with him. She was stunning, absolutely stunning. Wrapped seductively in a forest green dress that made her coloring look that much more vivid, she had the grace and bearing of a model.

And then Cully recognized her. The woman was Serena Woolsey.

Her attention was brought back to Randolph, who stood awkwardly at her side, his long face appearing to form a question mark. "Is something wrong?" he asked.

She realized that he hadn't yet noticed who else was at the party, and also that he was waiting to escort her inside. She allowed him to do so. "No," she demurred.

Her suspicions regarding Brandon's motives for taking her out the previous night began to surface again in light of the way Serena was pressing herself against Brandon's arm. A tiny spark of jealousy flickered through Cully as she realized how breathtakingly beautiful Serena really was. Oh well, none of this was truly her concern. Besides, Brandon could just be innocently escorting Serena, much as she had allowed Randolph to bring her.

But somehow Cully doubted it. This was apparently no simple client-lawyer relationship. None of *her* clients ever hung on her arm like that, Cully thought.

"Oh, here's Mrs. McBain," Randolph said, sounding relieved at having found her.

Mrs. McBain, a gray-haired, rather fleshy woman, was wrapped in a bolt of royal blue cloth that purported to be high fashion. Cully had no doubt that the dress bore someone's designer label on it, as well as a price tag that ran into four figures. Just proves that taste can't always be bought, Cully thought dryly.

"Wonderful!" the plump woman exclaimed, clapping her hands together. "You came after all," she said to Randolph. "And this is . . . ?" she asked brightly, her small eyes peering at Cully in a friendly appraisal that told Cully she had passed the test—whatever the requirements might have been.

"My lawyer," Randolph answered. "Yvette Culhane."

"My, my, it seems to be an evening for lawyers," the woman said, fluttering. She looked about. "Andrea is coming later?" she asked, inquiring after his sister.

Randolph shook his head. "No, she sends her regrets."

I'll bet, Cully thought. The girl was probably home, washing her hair.

"What a pity," Mrs. McBain clucked.

Cully took the opportunity to pick up a glass of wine from a nondescript butler walking by with a tray. She was definitely going to need it, she thought.

She didn't realize how much so until their hostess went on, squeezing Randolph's hand with what appeared to be secret glee. "I have an ulterior motive for inviting you, you know," she said to Randolph.

He nodded again. "I know. I've got my checkbook right here," he told her, taking it out with his free hand. It tumbled to his feet.

"No, no, dear boy. *That* motive everyone knows about." She looked toward Cully like a fellow conspirator. "I'm planning a reconciliation," she bubbled.

Cully immediately understood the woman's words. Her eyes darted back where Brandon had been standing. He was still watching them, amusement highlighting his rugged features. When he caught her eye, he winked. Then Serena called his attention to something and he turned away. Cully took a deep breath, fortifying herself. Things were getting complicated.

She turned her attention back to Randolph, who was having trouble comprehending what Mrs. McBain was driving at. But then, he still hadn't seen Brandon, Cully thought—or Brandon's date.

As lawyers for the two opposing sides, she and Brandon had already gone through the formality of attempting a reconciliation by way of settling on a compromise. Neither side had been willing to give in, and that had been that.

"Mrs. McBain, I'm not sure if this is wise," Cully began.

But Mrs. McBain didn't seem to even hear her as she all but propelled Randolph in Serena's direction. Cully chose to follow at a distance.

Serena's expression turned from a smile to a hard frown as her eyes mirthlessly washed over her younger brother; then she looked at their hostess accusingly.

"Agatha, how could you?" she demanded.

Randolph seemed far less composed than his sister. His round, button eyes appeared almost to pop out as he stared at Serena. Cully wondered if he were trying to summon a look of indignation. If so, he was failing miserably.

"I was only trying to get you two to forgive and forget. Court cases can be so . . . so tasteless, my dear," the older woman said, looking from one estranged sibling to the other.

A small group was beginning to form around them, Cully noticed, curious as to what the outcome of this orchestrated encounter would be.

"Not where money's concerned," Serena said, a sly

smile on her lips. Cully noticed that never once did she let go of Brandon's arm. "Of course, I'm willing to avoid a scandal if my dear brother over there would just agree to give me my share." Serena looked around at the various people gathered about her. "I only want what's mine," she said, her lower lip pouting appealingly.

"You gave that up when you refused to listen to father's wishes and walked out on him," Randolph rasped, for once managing to look truly angry.

So he did have some backbone after all, Cully thought. Good for him.

Serena looked as if she wanted to scratch his eyes out. "Daddy and I had our differences," she said airily, "but he would never have left me out of the will if you and Andrea hadn't poisoned his mind against me!"

Brandon put a restraining arm around Serena's nearly bare shoulders. "Now, Serena, you can't air the case here in public," he chided tactfully. "All this will be worked out in court," he assured her. He looked at Cully. "Won't it, counselor?" he asked.

Cully smiled meaningfully as she drew herself up a little taller. "Yes, it will, counselor. You can be sure of it," she promised.

"Now, now, I didn't bring you all together to fight." Mrs. McBain was flustered, looking unhappy that her plan had failed.

"Of course you didn't," Brandon said kindly, taking the lead expertly. "Why don't we get on with the plight of the birds, Aggie?" he urged kindly.

Aggie? Never in a million years would she have attached that nickname to the woman, Cully thought, looking at her imposing bulk. Was Brandon on familiar terms with every woman? Cully wondered. She wouldn't put it past him, she thought, taking Randolph from the line of battle. But in this case, she decided, looking over her shoulder at Brandon, it wasn't going to help him one bit.

The remainder of the evening, which consisted of a rather sumptuous dinner and some very mild entertainment rendered by a five-piece orchestra, proved rather awkward. It was as if everyone in the room were aware of the two enemy camps into which the Woolsey family had been split—everyone, that was, except for Brandon.

Mrs. McBain, in her attempts at reconciliation, had seated the two couples next to one another. Randolph was deeply dismayed and Serena made snide comments. Cully and Brandon were left to sort out the matter.

"No reason why we can't all be civil," Brandon said cheerfully, flashing a brilliant smile at Serena, which Cully was quick to take note of.

"I don't want to sit next to her," Randolph whispered urgently to Cully, his eyes darting toward his sister. There was nothing left to do but trade places with him.

Brandon, she noted out of the corner of her eye, was doing the same with Serena, so Cully wound up with Brandon sitting at her elbow. All through the meal she was very, very aware of his presence. Most of his conversation was directed at Serena, which annoyed Cully, even though she tried to talk herself out of it.

At one point, during a lull, Cully suddenly felt his hand on her thigh. When she glared at him, he merely smiled. "Anything wrong, Evie?" he asked innocently. He took a sip of his red wine.

"You've got your hand on my knee," she whispered between barely moving lips, hoping that no one else heard her.

"Sorry," he said easily. He seemed in no hurry to withdraw it, instead beginning a languid, stroking gesture that wrought havoc with her nervous system. "Wrong knee," he apologized.

Now what was that supposed to mean? Had he meant to touch Serena's leg instead, or was he just being cute? Cully turned her attention back to her pressed duck.

After dinner couples began to drift away from the table toward the area that had been set aside for dancing. The orchestra played slow-paced numbers obviously intended to soothe the atmosphere and put everyone in the frame of mind to give away money.

"Care to dance?"

Cully looked up from her strawberry parfait. A glance to her right told her that Mrs. McBain was doing a far better job of getting Randolph to talk than she had managed. The chair to Brandon's left was empty. Serena was gone.

"Serena is renewing some old acquaintances," Brandon told her, following the direction of her gaze.

"Is mind-reading part of your bag of tricks?" Cully asked, rising.

Brandon took her hand. Immediately she responded to the warm pressure. "I have no bag of tricks," he told her. "I'm just a humble lawyer."

"There's nothing humble about you," she informed him.

He grinned in response. "Oh, but there is, especially when I'm in your presence." He slipped his arm about her shoulders and held her other hand against his chest as his body began to sway with the music.

As they danced, Cully had to fight to keep from being overwhelmed by a feeling of being on pins and needles. Her whole body, molded against his, was fighting her. It was as if he were part of her, which, of course, was ridiculous, she told herself.

Brandon's arm held her to him, a smile creeping over his lips as her breasts pressed against his chest. Cully tried not to notice, but her resolve left as Brandon's hand slipped down to rest comfortably just below her waist. His fingers kept brushing over the upper portion of her buttocks.

"Your hand," Cully warned.

"Yes it is, isn't it?" he replied innocently.

The man was maddening. "Remove it or lose it," she told him through clenched teeth, trying hard not to cause a scene.

"Well, since it's the hand I use to sign my checks, I'd better obey."

"Very wise of you."

His hand went back to a more conventional position. "I must admit, I liked you better last night."

"I don't doubt that you did," she said archly, feeling her body bend with his. Delightful sensations that had nothing to do with her conscious mind began to roam freely through her.

"You were softer then," he said, whispering the words into her hair as she laid her head against his chest.

His breath made her warmer. She tried to steel herself. After all, people were probably watching them. "All the better for you to work with, right?"

"Have you that low an opinion of yourself?" he asked. She opened her mouth to reply, but he pressed her closer to him at that moment, temporarily making her lose her breath. "Can't you imagine that a man might want to take you out just because you make him think of nothing else?" he asked, his eyes searching her face.

"My self-esteem is alive and well, thank you," she answered. "But I truly doubt that anything could make you forget everything else."

"Then you don't know me very well," he told her, his voice just a touch serious. "Get to know me well," he urged. He almost sounded sincere.

But at that moment Serena came to claim both him and the rest of the dance. Cully gave him up, returning to the safety that Randolph's blandness offered her.

She could feel Brandon's eyes following her back to the table.

Cully decided that she needed some air. Maybe a stroll around the grounds would help alleviate the hot pounding of her blood. Just as she neared the terrace, another couple wandered out, and the ensuing wave of cold air from the opened doors halted Cully in her tracks. To cool off was one thing, to catch cold was another. She went off in search of the butler in order to find out where her wrap had been taken.

She found the man over in the corner, preparing a new round of hors d'oeuvres to be brought out.

"Excuse me. Could you tell me where my wrap is?" Cully asked, lightly tapping the man on the shoulder.

"Is madam leaving?" the tall man asked imperiously.

"No, just intent on getting a breath of fresh air," Cully replied. She looked around to see if she could spot Randolph to let him know she was stepping out for a moment.

"I shall fetch it for you."

"No, please," she said, looking back at him. "That's all right. I'm quite used to getting my own things. If you'll just tell me where it is . . ." Her voice trailed off, leaving a space for him to jump in and tell her.

The butler looked at her as if she were trying to cut him out of his job, then replied coldly, "Upstairs. Second room to your right."

Cully nodded her thanks and went up. The house, she decided, could double for a museum. And, despite its rich furnishing, it felt about as cozy as one. Everything had an austere air to it. All the portraits that lined the walls appeared to be passing judgment on her. She made her way quickly past them to the room the butler had indicated.

The room she found was surprisingly small. At least, it looked small in the dim light coming in from the hall. Cully felt along the wall, her fingers brushing against the fine, raised design on the wallpaper as she tried to find the light switch. She could make out the bed, which was overloaded with expensive fur coats and jackets. She wondered if her simple shawl was being crushed somewhere on the bottom.

A hand went over hers, stopping her from turning the light on. She smelled his enticing cologne before she turned around to face him.

"Cozy little room for an encounter," Brandon said, his presence seeming to fill the entire room.

"Do your encountering with someone else," Cully retorted.

It didn't appear as if he were going to be put off by that, she thought as he stepped toward her. He took her hand prisoner. Cully backed away instinctively, the prey trying to escape the hunter. Her high heel caught on the rug, throwing her off balance. She fell backwards, landing on top of someone's ermine coat. Soft fur surrounded her. To her horror, rather than help her up, Brandon lay down right along with her. The hard contours of his body seemed to fit neatly against her soft ones.

"Ms. Culhane, I presume." It sounded as if he was mocking her.

"You presume too damn much," she snapped.

"Ah, but the body feels the same," he told her. "I recall the feeling from last night."

"Get off me," she demanded, "or else—"

"Or else what?" he asked mischievously. Even in the dim light, she could see his eyes sparkling as he looked down at her.

Or else I'll succumb, she thought in despair. She tried to wriggle free, but all she seemed to do was bring herself more firmly against him. It also aroused her.

"Brandon . . ." she warned, trying to push him off.

"Right here," he murmured, just before he kissed her.

The kiss was her undoing. Every part of her body mutinied, responding to him even more intently than it had at the restaurant. She wanted him. Knowing the full folly of such an act, she still wanted him. It proved to Cully that she was not the master of her soul the way she had thought she was.

Brandon's lips left hers, but for the moment she had no strength with which to protest the assault upon her throat that followed. She had never known she could have such an erotic response to being kissed on the hollow of her throat. She found out. It seemed to be a night for finding out a lot of things about herself, most of which distressed her, because they all involved Brandon.

"You know," he said, raising his head and looking at her again, his voice just a touch breathless, "I have a bearskin rug up at my cabin that you might fit on very nicely."

His teasing, light tone gave her a chance to try to rally her senses, to pull back from the hot passion he was awakening in her. But she doubted that she would have been able to make him release her had it not been for the sound of approaching voices. Someone was coming into the room!

"Get off me," she pleaded, straining to see who was coming.

"What will you give me?" he teased.

"A well-placed kick if you don't," she threatened in near panic. It wouldn't do for anyone to see her like this—especially Randolph. How would he feel, seeing his lawyer lying on an ermine coat with the opposition on top of her? Certainly not very confident, to say the least.

"You have such a way with words," Brandon quipped, finally lifting his weight from her.

Cully sprang to her feet, afraid that he would have a change of heart. She quickly brushed at the wrinkles in her outfit, hoping that she didn't look too mussed.

"Yes, I do," she snapped. "And you'll learn all about it at the trial," she told him coolly, lifting her head high as she walked out of the room.

Cully's mind was a blur during the fund raising

portion of the evening, and she hardly remembered Randolph bringing her home. All that seemed to stay with her was the look in Brandon's eyes when he had urged her to get to know him better—that and the gnawing feeling that if she weren't careful, she was going to regret all this.

7

Brandon turned up in court the next day.

Cully had a very cut and dried case that morning and it was easily won. There was no real challenge to it. The other side seemed only to go through the formalities; they put up no real struggle.

The only time Cully became at all unsure of herself was when she was packing her briefcase and looked up, sensing rather than hearing someone come up behind her. She turned on her heel just as Brandon uttered the words, "Very good."

She looked at him, both startled and surprised at finding him there. As far as she knew, he had no connections with either side. This well-dressed man in his British-styled Persian blue suit was studying her technique firsthand, she realized. He was going to leave nothing to chance.

"I always am," she replied coolly, pushing her papers into her briefcase with a little more force than necessary.

"That remains to be seen," he told her. She wondered if he was merely talking about their pending case or something more. "Buy you lunch?" he asked amicably.

"Why are you always trying to feed me?" she wanted to know, snapping the lid of the briefcase shut.

"Maybe I'd like to have you eating out of the palm of my hand . . . or something like that." His eyes danced mischievously.

"Never happen," she informed him, still polite, still distant. But she had to work at keeping the smile off her lips. Somehow she couldn't stay annoyed around him any longer, no matter how justifiable that annoyance was. He was definitely a charmer, no doubt about it. "Besides," she added, "I have to get back to the office."

"All work and no play . . ." he began, eyeing the way her deep rust suit accented her figure. The straight, tapered skirt managed to show off her supple, slim hips with each move she made.

"—leads to winning cases," she concluded. "Well, if you'll excuse me, I have a full calendar waiting for me," she said, trying to get past him.

Brandon followed her out through the double doors of the courtroom and down the long, well-lit hallway. "Can I give you a lift?" he offered as she came to a halt before the elevator bank.

"I prefer walking," she told him.

"Fine, then I'll—"

"No," she said, stepping into the elevator and

quickly pressing the "close" button. "I wouldn't let you leave your poor car unattended."

The last thing she saw was his mouth opening in further protest as the doors closed.

Cully smiled to herself. She had managed to outmaneuver him. Score one for her side, she thought.

She was feeling quite happy with herself by the time she got back to work. She crossed the street toward the building that housed the offices of Abernathy, Kilt & Dale. The edifice looked like a giant cube of sugar to her, catching the bright rays of the sun and gleaming invitingly. It was going to be a glorious day.

But somehow it slid downhill after that. Sheer doggedness carried her through her rather heavy work load, and she saw three clients, including one woman who wanted to rewrite her will for a fourth time; then the phone rang. It was Randolph Woolsey, asking to make up for the previous night.

"None of last night was your fault," Cully said, doodling absently on the only available place left on her calendar, the border.

"Still, it was rather unpleasant, and I think I owe you a peaceful evening." He sounded rather eager to please, she thought.

Peaceful, as in dull, Cully interpreted. Out loud, she asked, "What did you have in mind?"

"There's this cultural tea being given at the Art Institute for private contributors. I've been quite generous with them in the past . . ."

So they're springing for a cup of tea for you and a date, Cully ended silently. "Um, Randolph, I'm not quite sure if I can make it . . ." she began, trying to beg off. It sounded like a very boring evening.

"I'll be a perfect gentleman," Randolph assured her quickly.

Cully caught herself smiling. Nothing else had crossed her mind. Well, what did she want, bells and banjos each time she went out with a man? She deserved to celebrate, didn't she? She had won a case that morning, not to mention that she had managed to give Brandon the slip.

Brandon. The mere thought of him quickened her pulse and made her decision for her. "I'll be happy to attend with you," she told Randolph.

"Wonderful, wonderful." She could almost hear him beaming on the other end. "Six-thirty all right with you?" he asked.

That gave her an hour and a half after she got home. She would probably need all of ten minutes to get ready. "Yes," she replied.

As she hung up a strange emptiness mingled with disappointment went through her. She pushed it aside and had June send in her next client. He turned out to be a man with a list of bequests a mile long and an equally long, boring story to go with each one of them. Cully had trouble keeping her eyes open.

But something happened at four-thirty, when she took a call from Madge, that opened them for her.

"Evie, I'm sorry to bother you at work," the woman apologized.

Cully could hear the breathless tone in Madge's voice. "What's the matter?"

"It's Timmy," the woman told her, her voice hesitant, as if she wasn't sure calling Cully had been a good idea.

Cully's mind, normally so cool, began to imagine all sorts of things. The first thing that burst upon her was the accident Timmy had been in four years earlier. She had seen him struck down by a hit-and-run driver right before her eyes.

"What about Timmy?" she asked, fighting to remain calm.

"He hasn't come home yet. I didn't know whether or not to call. It's just that he's usually so prompt . . ."

"He didn't call?" Cully asked, holding on to her pen in a tightening grip. Her thumbnail dug into her forefinger. Of course he hadn't called. Would Madge have sounded that way if he had?

"No. No, I . . . What do you want me to do?"

"Nothing. I'm coming home," Cully said, her heart pounding nervously. She hung up without any further words.

She didn't like it. Timmy was usually a good boy. If he was going to be the slightest bit late, he always called her or Madge. Madge stayed with him every day after school until Cully came home. Cully tried to make sure that Timmy never felt neglected. There always had to be somebody around to lend him emotional support if he needed it. Madge fit the bill perfectly.

He was all right, she told herself firmly as she stuffed a few things into her briefcase. She glanced at the case she was working on, undecided for a moment as to whether or not to take it with her. If everything was all right, then she'd be going out with Randolph shortly, and that promised to be an early evening. Might as well get some work done. She had just picked up the file when she heard the phone ring in the outer office. Now what? she thought impatiently.

Her buzzer went off, and she flipped the switch on the intercom. "Yes?"

"It's Brandon Fitzhugh."

The man had lousy timing, she thought cryptically. Had he called an hour ago, she would have spoken with him. Something within her was terribly drawn to the velvet sound of his voice, but now she had no time to spend indulging herself. "Tell him I've left for the day," Cully instructed her. "Oh, and June . . ."

"Yes?"

"I *have* left for the day. I'm going home."

"Anything wrong?" June asked.

"I hope not," Cully answered. She switched off the intercom. "I hope not," she repeated in a whisper.

She got home just a little after five. She hadn't waited for the bus or bothered to hail a cab. At this time of day they were far too slow for her. The streets were filled with rush-hour traffic, cars all lined up bumper to bumper, all moving an inch at a time, their drivers impatient to get home. Cully made better time walking the twenty blocks.

Even though she was in excellent shape, she was out of breath when she reached her apartment building, still walking at a fast clip. She leaned against the side of the elevator wall as she rode up.

He was all right, she told herself for the dozenth time. He was home right now, waiting for her.

But he wasn't. One look at Madge's face as she walked in told her that.

"No call?" Cully asked.

Madge shook her head.

Cully went straight to the phone book on the ornate oriental hutch by the door, for once not looking with pride at the deep, gleaming shine of the dark wood. She began flipping through the suede-bound book until she came to the letter *T*, where she kept an up-to-date list of all of Timmy's friends.

"There's probably nothing to worry about," Madge told her, coming up behind her and watching her dial. The older woman clutched a handkerchief in her hand.

"Of course not," Cully said hollowly as the phone rang on the other end. "He's probably declaring his independence by not phoning home," she said.

No, that wasn't like Timmy. But lately something had been on his mind. She had been able to see it, sense it. He just hadn't opened up to her. He was changing, growing up, she thought with a twinge of sadness.

The phone call yielded nothing. Neither did the next, nor the next. Five calls later Cully still had nothing to go on. Timmy had left school at the same time everyone else had—alone. One boy said that he had seemed intent on going somewhere.

Where? she wondered. Where would he want to go? And why hadn't he called, unless . . . ? She bit her lip. For the first time, she was in a quandary as to what to do next.

"Maybe we should call the police?" Madge suggested.

Cully shook her head, the damp curls above her forehead making a tight little crown about her head. "He's only been missing for a little over two and a half hours. Maybe I'm overreacting. I don't know if—"

Just then the front door opened. A flood of relief and parental anger filled every pore of her body as Cully saw her son come in.

"Where have you been?" she demanded, hugging

him to her. At the same time, she wanted to shake him for what he had just put her through.

"With me."

Cully looked up to see Brandon standing in her doorway. Her eyes narrowed in confusion. Why had Timmy been with him? "Is this true, Timmy?" she asked.

The blond head nodded. "I went to see him after school," he said, looking a little hesitant in front of his mother. Then his eyes shifted back to Brandon, and he looked bright and eager again.

Cully bit her lip. She was surprised that Timmy even knew where to find Brandon. What was going on there? "Why did you go to see him?" she wanted to know.

Timmy shrugged. "I hadda talk to him," he said, his voice indicating that he recognized her displeasure. He looked a little uncertain now.

"But why?" she asked again, bending down to his level. "If you had a problem, you could have come to me," she said, putting her hand on his shoulder and searching his face. "You know you can tell me anything." It wasn't as if she were unavailable, she told herself. She had let her son know in no uncertain terms that he always came first in her life. Why was he acting this way?

Timmy shrugged his thin shoulders again, looking down at the plush carpet beneath his blue and white sneakers, then up at Brandon's face, as if for support. "It was man-talk," he said finally.

Man-talk. What kind of nonsense was Brandon filling his head with? she thought, looking at the man accusingly. Timmy was a seven-year-old *boy*. What sort of "man-talk" could he possibly be capable of?

He was still too young for girls. He thought they were "icky," to use his term. She was utterly baffled.

"All right," she said calmly, trying to accept the explanation. "But that still doesn't excuse you for not calling," she told Timmy. Her eyes held him fast as she looked into the guileless face. "Honey, we were worried sick about you. Why didn't you call Aunt Madge or me and tell us you wanted to go see him?"

"He was afraid you'd say no," Brandon told her, finally cutting short his silence and putting a protective hand on Timmy's shoulder. Timmy glanced up at him. Cully saw both gratitude and hero worship in her son's pale green eyes.

"Why didn't you send him home?" Cully demanded. Surely he couldn't be so insensitive as to not know that she would be worried about the whereabouts of a seven-year-old boy.

"Because he wanted to talk," Brandon told her simply. "But I did try to call you," he told her. "You weren't in."

Cully caught her breath, momentarily embarrassed. She rose to her feet. Then he hadn't called to ask her out. He had called to tell her that Timmy was with him. The flame within her eyes flickered for a moment, then became subdued. "I thought you were calling . . ." Her voice trailed off, as she realized that she was admitting to having been there when he called.

"Then you were in," Brandon said, his smile mocking her slightly. "See, you should always take your phone calls."

Cully turned to her son. "Timmy, go wash up," she instructed the boy.

He looked hesitant about leaving the room. "Am I being punished?" he asked, his voice slightly worried.

"No, not this time," Cully replied. "Since you did try to call me, it's not your fault that I was worried."

A bright gleam of a smile returned to the small face as Timmy fairly bounced out of the room.

"Why were you so worried?" Brandon asked, glancing at his watch. "I know he's only seven, but he's not that late. You were white as a sheet when we walked in."

"Timmy was in an accident when he was a little boy. I almost lost him. I have a tendency to overreact when I don't know where he is," Cully confessed before she had time to stop and think. Why was she explaining herself to him? There was no need to be telling him all this.

She saw the light of sympathy come into his intense blue eyes. "I'm sorry; I didn't know. It must have been very rough on you," he said softly.

She shrugged. She didn't want his pity. "I managed."

"Ever the trouper," he said dryly.

She didn't know if he was mocking her or not, but she suddenly realized that she was running out of time. Randolph would be there soon.

A sneeze from Madge suddenly reminded her that she had forgotten all about asking her to babysit.

"Oh, Madge, I have to go out tonight," Cully said. "Can you stay with Timmy?"

Madge nodded, her nose buried for the moment in a delicately embroidered handkerchief that was getting quite a workout.

"Who with?" Brandon asked.

"What?" Cully asked, turning to look in his direction.

"Who are you going out with?" Brandon repeated.

"Randolph Woolsey, if it's any business of yours," she said shortly. Who did he think he was, turning her life upside down, charming her son—invading her dreams? This kind of thing had to stop.

Brandon shook his head, as if in disbelief. "You can do better than that," he told her.

"I haven't the slightest idea what you mean," she said coolly. "He asked me out to a tea at the Art Institute, and I'm going."

"A tea?" Brandon echoed with a laugh. He drew nearer to her, making her feel breathless and heady. "You're much too vibrant a woman to take to a tea," he scoffed. "You should be wined and dined," he murmured softly, his words almost gliding off her skin. They made her feel warm with the promises that lay beneath them.

She tried to shake herself free of the spell he was weaving. "And plied with liquor?" she added dryly. "This is just an evening out," she informed him. "Not a prelude to seduction."

"Glad to hear that," Brandon told her with a smile.

She turned on her heel and hurried to her room, needing to get away from those eyes that seemed to burn themselves into her brain.

As she quickly changed her clothes, she tried not to think about the reaction she was having to Brandon. She put on a terracotta-colored shirt-waist dress and dug up matching shoes from the bottom of her walk-in closet. Cully loved shoes, and they were the only real indulgence she allowed herself. She had a matching pair of shoes for every outfit she owned.

Patting her hair, Cully decided to leave it up. No sense in encouraging Randolph, she told herself. She knew that she looked more sensual with her hair down. After the tea she was politely going to refuse any other plans he might come up with. Dating was a waste of time, she thought. She had more than enough in her life with Timmy and her work.

All the while the memory of Brandon's eyes haunted her.

The real thing haunted her as she came out of her bedroom again.

"Fast," he observed, glancing at his watch. She had taken all of twelve minutes to get ready.

"I don't like to waste time," she said, looking at him make himself comfortable on her sofa. Did he think he was settling in?

"Neither do I," he told her.

She didn't have time to explore that comment, she told herself. Randolph was due any minute, and she didn't want him seeing Brandon there. It might look like collusion to the other man. After all, she was going to be facing Brandon in court soon.

"Shouldn't you be going?" she wanted to know, standing before him with her hands on her hips.

"Tim and I haven't finished our talk yet," Brandon said by way of explanation. "He's in the kitchen, getting us a sandwich."

Cully closed her eyes, willing herself to have strength. "Madge," she said, turning to the sniffling woman who was sitting next to Brandon. "Am I putting you out?" she asked, suddenly realizing that Madge was suffering from a cold. In her concern about Timmy, and then her confusion with Brandon, her poor aunt had been lost in the shuffle.

But the woman shook her head, waving a dismissing hand at Cully. "No, it's all right," she said, her voice a shade deeper than it normally was. "Just a simple cold. The weather changed too abruptly for me," she diagnosed. "You go and have a good time." But her words indicated that she didn't see how Cully could, inasmuch as Brandon wasn't accompanying her.

Just then Cully heard the doorbell. "I'll be home early," she promised.

"See that you are," Brandon called after her.

Cully grabbed her purse and eased herself out the door, not trusting herself to reply.

The tea went about as she had expected. It was uncommonly boring, and Cully had all she could do not to start yawning early in the evening. Randolph, though, appeared to be right in his element.

Some bulbous-looking man held them both captive for over forty-five minutes, giving a dissertation on the chiaroscuro technique employed by Rembrandt. Cully had never found paintings as dull as she did that night. Without meaning to, she caught herself comparing how she felt then to the way she had felt when Brandon had taken her to the Japanese restaurant. No, that really wasn't fair. Comparing Brandon to Randolph was like comparing the sun to a yellow crayon. The similarity ended with the common color.

"I really am very tired," Cully confessed to Randolph after three hours had dragged by. If she didn't get home soon, she was going to fall asleep right there, with her punch glass dangling from her hand. She had already consumed nine tiny glasses for lack of anything else to do.

Randolph immediately took the hint and had his car

brought around, then thanked the people in charge for an exhilarating evening. To each his own, Cully thought wearily. She was just glad to be leaving.

"Where would you like to go tomorrow night?" Randolph asked as the chauffeur drove them back to her apartment.

Cully smiled. "I have a lot of work to do on your case," she said politely but firmly.

"Oh." Randolph appeared crestfallen, his sharp chin pointing down the neatly arranged line of buttons on his brown vest. "Does that mean that I won't be seeing you anymore?"

"You'll be seeing a lot of me," Cully told him. "I have more questions to ask, and there are a few more depositions to be made." She kept it all very business-like and hoped he'd understand.

He did. "Then I'll walk you to your door and thank you for a pleasant evening," he said graciously.

"That would be nice," Cully said as the car came to a stop before the awning-covered entrance to her apartment building.

It was just as well that Randolph hadn't asked to come in with her, because the first thing Cully saw as she opened her door was Brandon.

8

"What are you doing here?" Cully demanded impatiently.

Brandon was sitting comfortably on her sofa, his jacket carelessly discarded over the back. Next to him was the sleeping form of her son. The television set droned softly in the background, a science fiction movie going through its mechanical paces. Science fiction movies were a favorite with Timmy.

"I'm keeping him company," Brandon answered simply, nodding at Timmy.

"Where's Madge?" she wanted to know, looking around.

"I sent her home."

"You what?" She struggled to keep her voice from waking Timmy. Why did this man feel compelled to take charge of her life? Why couldn't she make him go away?

"Her cold sounded pretty bad to me. I thought she'd be better off in bed. We'd all be better off in bed," he murmured. Before she had a chance to retort, he went on. "Besides, I had nothing pressing to do tonight, and Tim looked like he needed my company. Quite a boy you have here," he said.

She glanced down at the top of the blond head that leaned so comfortably against Brandon. "Yes, I know," she said with warm affection.

"You said you raised him all by yourself?" he asked.

Cully sighed, putting her purse on the coffee table. "His father didn't even want visiting rights. I don't think he wanted to have anything to do with either one of us," she said quietly, bending over to take off Timmy's sneakers.

"What a fool," she heard Brandon mutter under his breath. She stopped what she was doing and glanced up, her eyes meeting his for a moment. "Here, let me help," he offered, rising and picking the boy up in his arms. "Which way's the bedroom?" he asked. "His," he added, his eyes twinkling.

"That way," Cully replied, pointing to the left and following him.

They walked into the small room, which gave clear testimony to Timmy's passion for science fiction. There were posters of recent block-buster movies, various science fiction books strewn about and a stuffed toy that sat perched upon his desk, smiling benignly. Cully pulled back the downy comforter from Timmy's bed and Brandon laid him gently down.

Then he leaned back against the bureau, his arms crossed over his chest, watching Cully's every move as she went through the ritual of preparing Timmy for bed. It was such a domestic scene, she thought, glancing at Brandon as she went about her task. A pang went through her as she admitted to herself that perhaps this was something she did indeed miss.

"Once he got going," Brandon said, finally breaking the silence, "I couldn't get him to stop talking."

Cully shook her head as she went to the bureau to pull out a pair of clean pajamas. Brandon slid his trim hips out of her way only after she made a motion toward him. "Timmy should know better than to bother strangers with his problems. I'm sorry."

"He wasn't bothering me," Brandon protested, following. He lifted the boy's shoulders as Cully slipped on the pajama top and snapped it closed over his small chest. "Besides, I'd like to be a friend—a close family friend."

Their eyes met and held for a moment. She wished she could read what was behind that sparkling blue mist. "How close?" she heard herself asking.

"Very, very close," he said huskily, his fingers wrapping about her hand.

Unnerved, Cully rose. "Here," she said, handing him the bottom of the set. "You can start being close by getting him out of his jeans and into these," she instructed, then left the room. It was getting too stifling for her.

She walked into the dimly lit living room, where she snapped off the TV and threw open a window that looked out onto a busy avenue. Headlights seared into the moonless night, throwing glaring strips of harsh light across the darkness. She took a deep breath of air to steady herself. It helped, but only for a moment.

"All tucked in," Brandon announced, coming back into the room. "Can I do the same for his mother?" he offered, his tone inviting and almost endearing.

She turned to look at him. If only he had come into her life as a man, not as a lawyer who would be opposing her, she thought with a wave of despair. How lost she could get in those arms. How she yearned to be held, to be made to feel like a vibrant woman again. Her ex-husband had made her feel less than a woman. She had gotten to the point where she felt undesirable, unattractive. It had taken a long while before she had regained her confidence. Her outward poise had stayed unaffected, but inside, where it counted, she had been hollow, shaky. She had worked hard at covering that up, even from herself. It had taken Brandon's kiss to remind her.

"I can tuck myself in, thank you," she said crisply. And then her voice softened. "And thank you for taking care of Timmy . . . and for listening to him," she said, coming away from the window.

"My pleasure," he told her, watching her every move. When she sat down on the sofa, he was right there beside her. "Besides," Brandon continued, "I like him, and I'm crazy about his mother."

"Uh-huh," Cully nodded. "You'll forgive me if I choose not to believe you."

"Why?" he asked innocently. The gentle ripples of his breath floated against her ear, stirring something to life within her that she was trying so hard to control. "He's really a neat boy."

"I meant the other part," she said with an effort. He was closing in on her. Why didn't she just push him away? Because you want him, that's why, her little voice accused her.

"Don't you think a man could be crazy about you?" he asked, taking her hand in his.

"I think you're only crazy about victory," she said. The hand—retrieve your hand, the small voice urged. The hand remained where it was, linking her to him, drawing the warmth from his strong fingertips into her own.

"That depends on what kind of victory you're talking about," he told her, running his other hand along her cheek, stroking it lovingly.

If only his eyes weren't so hypnotic, his smile so enticing, she thought desperately. Why couldn't he affect her like Randolph did? Or any other man, for that matter? Why did he have to be the special one?

"The kind of victory that would propel you into Serena's arms." Now where had that come from? But once she said it, she was glad. It took him aback. She wondered if it was guilt that momentarily flickered in his eyes. Usually she could judge people and their actions so well. But he was a mystery to her . . . or was she trying to make him one because she hoped that he *wasn't* only laying siege to her because of the Woolsey case?

"Serena?" he asked, dumbfounded. "I'd have to buy a ticket to get into her arms," he laughed.

"That's not the way it looked last night," she said.

"Oh?" he asked, interested. He snuggled closer. Cully tried to pull herself away . . . and was glad that the deepness of the sofa held her as much of a prisoner as his arm did. After all, it wasn't her fault. It was the couch's. "And just how did it look?"

"Like she was all over you," Cully replied. Was that really her, sounding like that? Someone would think that she was . . . jealous. "I'm sure that if you win your case, as you hope you will"—she emphasized "hope"—"you won't have to buy a ticket at all. You'll be first in line."

"Now, now, counselor, you're violating ethics here," he chided playfully. "We're not supposed to be discussing the case, remember?"

"I'm not discussing the case," she bristled. "I was only making an observation." The pompous oaf, did he presume to be more ethical than she was? Why—

"Shh," he said, putting his finger to her lips. "Not another word. Besides, Serena is only a client," he told her, bending his head slightly. The next thing she knew, she felt his lips skimming along the side of her neck. She drew her breath in sharply. "You've got nothing to be jealous of."

"Jealous? Why you . . . you . . ." Why wasn't her mouth working? She usually had a huge vocabulary at her disposal. What happened to her every time she was around him?

"Counselor," he said, raising his head to look at her for a moment.

"What?" she demanded hotly.

"Shut up."

And to insure that, he kissed her. His kiss, deceptively light and fluttery to begin with, nevertheless fanned an inner fire that had lain dormant for too long. Despite her common sense and a myriad of arguments to the contrary, there wasn't a moment's hesitation on Cully's part. She drank in the kiss as if it were intoxicating wine. And it only became more so as he smothered her senses, kissing her more ardently.

Cully felt herself being pressed against the side of the sofa. Brandon's arms cradled her, insulating her from all outside forces. How could she, in her haze, feel the total, distinct imprint of each of his fingers upon her body? And yet she could. She was utterly aware of each part of him as it came in contact with her.

His mouth worked over hers hungrily as he took more and more of what she offered there, absorbing sustenance and growing more demanding. The breaths Cully took in weren't deep enough to fortify her against the onslaught of his passion. She felt her common sense being shunted into the background.

Brandon's fervor grew. Was it possible? She felt his hands moving, spreading, massaging her back in larger and larger patterns as they crept ever forward until they touched the sides of her breasts.

Cully felt an explosion go off within her. She raised her arms about his neck, her fingers grabbing a little of the thick, luxurious hair that lay against his collar. It was all she could do to keep from crying, "Yes, touch me, please touch me."

But there was no need for supplication. He *was* touching her, touching her at first so reverently that, had it not been for the burning fire that grew higher with each slight pass, she would have doubted that his hands were there at all. But they were. They were.

Ever so gently, Brandon cupped his hands beneath her breasts, still shielded by her bra and her dress. But by and by the neckline of the dress parted, and his fingers deftly worked their way beneath the last flimsy barriers. He lifted one breast slightly, bending his head to cover the silken skin with a flurry of kisses, making her crave more, ever more.

She became aware that only one hand was at work

there. The other had slipped under the skirt of her dress and was now stroking her leg. The increasingly large circles came closer and closer to a danger zone.

Her breath ragged, her mind fighting with her emotions, Cully tried to push him away. But there was no strength in her arms. The sensations he created felt so wonderful. All of her pulsated as the pattern he stroked on her inner thigh grew smaller and more intense. He was going to take her right there, right then. . . .

"Brandon, please," she rasped. She felt as if she didn't have enough air to manage even those words.

"Anything," he promised, lifting his head. She saw nothing but raw desire in his eyes. Desire that matched her own.

"We can't . . . I can't . . ."

"Hush," he told her. "I'll be gentle."

As if she needed assurance of that. Gentle? His every movement was as considerate as it was arousing. She hadn't thought him capable of that. She had thought that a man like Brandon would take his pleasure where he could, satisfying only himself. But he seemed bent on giving her pleasure. His words from their first meeting came back to her. *I don't use women, I enjoy them.*

"Not here," she begged, trying to turn her head in the direction of her son's room but finding it increasingly difficult to pull her eyes away from his. "Timmy . . ."

It was really all she needed to say. Brandon drew in his breath as if to pull back his own desire. He nodded. "Okay." The tone of the single word was enough to give evidence of his fierce, short struggle. "But only if you promise to go out with me tomorrow night," he said. "I need that to hold me over," he told her, his eyes strangely serious. "Otherwise, counselor . . ." His voice trailed off. The sensuous bend of his mouth said it all.

"All right," she agreed, sitting up and trying to pull her senses together. "But to a public place," she cautioned.

He grinned. "You plan to sell tickets to this?" he asked.

She flushed. "No," she said. Why wasn't her voice as steady as his? she thought, annoyed with herself. "So that this won't happen again."

Brandon stayed her hand as she went to rebutton her blouse. For one short moment he gazed on her exposed, trembling flesh. A deep blush sprang to her cheeks, a blush that only he could bring out. She all but yanked the material out of his hand. "If you're through taking inventory . . ." she said, embarrassed.

"Lady, I've only begun," he murmured. But he rose obligingly, smoothing down his shirt and rebuttoning his vest, which, she realized, *she* must have unbuttoned. The cut of the vest brought out the trimness of his waist. As her eyes took in his figure, gliding over it with approval, she saw the evidence of her own effect on Brandon. It placated her annoyed feelings to see that he was as affected as she was by what had just happened between them.

"You're staring," he said. The grin was in his voice as well as on his face.

This time the blush must have gone to the roots of her hair, and she passionately wished she had an olive complexion to hide behind, instead of one that was so delicate and white.

He crooked his finger under her chin and raised her

eyes to his. "Are you sure you want me to go?" he asked softly.

"I was never so sure of anything in my life," she said, hoping she sounded convincing. If he pressed his advantage, she wasn't sure that she could stop him.

"Have it your way, counselor," Brandon said, picking up his jacket and slinging it carelessly over his shoulder. His forefinger was hooked into the neckline, anchoring the jacket in place. His hair was just slightly disheveled. It only served to enhance the total picture.

Cully's heart didn't stop pounding for several minutes after she had closed the door behind him.

When Brandon picked Cully up the next evening, she was dressed in a smart two-piece light gray suit and a feminine blue silk blouse.

"You look very nice," he commented as they left her building. "But it looks like you're planning to study some briefs, not go to see a play." Crisp brown leaves chased each other in a small, swirling circle across the dusty street as Brandon waved down a passing cab.

"A play?" Cully asked in surprise. She hadn't seen a play in so long. There never seemed to be enough time for that anymore.

"Would you rather study my briefs?" he whispered huskily into her ear.

Cully swallowed hard. "What play?" she asked, ignoring his question as he ushered her into the taxi.

"*Love's Comedy,*" he told her.

It was the hottest new musical in town. From what she had heard in the office and read in the paper, tickets were next to impossible to get. "How did you manage to get tickets to that?" she asked as the cab inched its way toward Monroe Street, where the theater was located.

"I have my ways," Brandon assured her, winking.

She was sure he had. "Do you always get your way?" she asked, trying to look ahead. But all she could think of was Brandon and the evening that lay before her—not so much the theater, but what was to follow.

"Always," he told her. It wasn't a boast, it was a stated fact.

She turned toward him, trying to keep a humorous lilt in her voice. "Something tells me I'm in trouble," she said.

"It's never been called that before," he commented, slipping his arm about her shoulders and pulling her closer.

She really was in trouble, her mind told her, unless she played the whole thing as a game. If he were bent on unnerving her—and part of her still believed that—then two could play that game. She told herself that if she were even half as desirable as he kept telling her she was, then she could get him to fall for her.

So, during the ride to the theater and at intermission, she was the soul of sparkling charm. She looked brightly into his face all through their dinner at an intimate little restaurant. Somewhere between after-dinner drinks and the dessert, when Brandon bent his head to kiss her, Cully reached his lips first, kissing him.

And somewhere just before the check came, Cully fell neatly into her own trap—Cully fell in love. Not willingly, not head over heels, just deeply. After her divorce there had been a terrible, heavy sadness in her heart that she had thought she would never overcome. When she had climbed out of the depths of the blackness her soul had sunk into, she had vowed that that was that. Never again. Never would she be so vulnerable again because of some man. And here she was, doing it all over again at the worst possible time and with the worst possible person.

But the question as to why she hadn't learned her lesson didn't occupy her mind for long. It was pushed aside by the excited glow that came whenever Brandon took her hand or even came close to her.

She stood outside the restaurant with him, feeling the chill in the evening air. Obviously the weatherman, who had promised her a warm night, had been wrong, she thought, shivering slightly.

"Cold?" Brandon asked as they waited for a gaunt doorman wrapped in green livery to hail a cab for them.

She nodded. "I should've worn a coat."

"Wear me instead," Brandon said, draping his arm about her and pulling her close to him. In reality the action should have done precious little to shield her from the rising winds that rustled the colorful leaves of the tree growing near the entrance. But as the heat of his body transferred itself to her, Cully grew warmer and warmer.

Brandon appeared to be sharing that sensation, judging by the smile he gave her. He was just about to kiss her, lifting her face toward his, when the doorman's whistle pierced the air. A taxi had appeared.

"Saved by the whistle," Brandon murmured into her hair.

A feeling of disappointment ran through her.

After ushering her gently into the cab, Brandon

eased his tall, robust form in next to her. He slammed the door and told the driver their destination.

Cully knitted her brows together for a second. That wasn't her address. She turned questioning eyes toward him.

"I thought we'd stop for a nightcap," he told her.

"Where?" she asked, a suspicious feeling crawling up lazily through the pit of her stomach.

"It's quiet. Tasteful. They only play the nicest music," he assured her. "You'll like it." It was a promise.

"Sounds heavenly. What's the name of this place?"

"I haven't named it yet."

"Your apartment?" she guessed.

"My apartment," he replied.

"I thought so." But she didn't refuse.

She should have. Oh, she should have, her logical mind hammered home to her as she walked into his living room. She was going to regret this evening before long, it nagged. But for some reason, she was reckless at the moment. She needed the attention he was paying her. Foolishly she told herself that she could stop this roller coaster at any time.

Cully looked around. Brandon seemed to be waiting for her verdict. "It's not as macho as I thought it would be."

He chuckled. "What did you expect?" he asked. "Lots of leather and whips hanging from the walls?" He went to turn on his stereo. Lush music filled the air.

"Something like that," Cully answered, walking over to the wall-to-ceiling bookcase that took up over three quarters of one wall. Only a small part of it was devoted to a television set and a stereo system. The rest was crammed with books. She ran her hand over a collection of poems by Byron. He was her favorite. She glanced at Brandon, trying to picture him reading it.

"Is this meant to impress people?" she asked lightly, fingering the gilded lettering that stood out against the deep green binding.

To her surprise, he began quoting "She walks in beauty like the night," as he slipped the book back in its place. His hand covered hers for a moment. It was evident that he meant the poem to be a tribute to her. "I read all my books," he told her finally.

"When do you have time for anything else?" she asked, stepping away from him. She felt like a moth drawn to a flame, beating her wings in an effort to draw away at the last minute, but doomed to fail.

"I manage," he murmured, following her to the sliding glass door. He opened it for her, and she stepped out on the small terrace. "If you're thinking of jumping," he teased, "we're twenty stories up."

Cully looked down. Below her the lights from whizzing automobiles mingled with one another. They held her attention only briefly. She felt his arms go about her waist, felt his hard chest against her back. "Come inside," he urged. "I thought you said you were cold?"

"Just a moment longer," she begged. "The night air might do me some good."

"Was it that bad for you?" he asked kindly, his eyes seeming to try to penetrate her thoughts.

"What?" she asked, startled.

"Your marriage."

She wondered if he really could see into her mind. "It taught me a lesson, I suppose," she said in a voice that she forced to sound removed. "Dick made me feel less than a woman because I couldn't fit into his preconceived notion of what a woman was. I really wanted to please him," she said distantly, staring up at the one star that was visible in the sky. "I really did. But there was that voice inside of me, that voice that kept urging me to amount to something, to make a difference in this world. I couldn't forsake that voice, and Dick couldn't live with where it took me."

Brandon slowly turned her around to face him. "He doesn't sound like much of a man if he was so easily threatened. Certainly not enough of a man to turn you against the whole species," he said softly. "Give us another chance, Evie." He kissed first one eyelid and then the other. Tantalizing pinpricks danced all through her. "Give yourself another chance," he urged, this time pulling her against himself as he kissed her hard on the mouth.

The lyric floating from the stereo speakers rang in her ears: "Too late to run for cover."

9

Brandon drew Cully back into the living room, shutting the terrace door behind her. "I won't be responsible for your getting pneumonia." He laughed softly, kissing the top of her head lovingly.

"It would be a way to win the case," she responded without even thinking. There it was. Just on the tip of her consciousness. No matter how she tried to dispel them, the doubts about his motives were there.

"To hell with the case," he said, seeking her lips out again. His voice sounded thick with yearning and desire. Could it be that he wanted her as much as she did him?

In a moment there was no room for thought, no room for anything except the flames that his hands produced in her. A desire and passion sprang up in response to his touch. His scorching, demanding mouth kissed her thoughts away, leaving room only for her to explore the wonderful sensations he was creating, delightful sensations that Cully had never known, even in the best of times.

Over and over again his hands gently kneaded her back, playing her, she realized, like a fine instrument—just as he had said. And for the moment she would play any tune he wanted. There was no question as to that. Every fiber of her being reacted to the growing pressures he was applying to her. She felt the sway of his body and thrilled to the way the hard contours seemed to fit into her own supple ones, as if she had been created just for him, just for this wondrous moment.

His movements excited her. Everything excited her, leading her to increasingly higher plateaus. She scarcely recognized herself. Did this passionate, wild creature live within the confines of the finely boned, reserved Yvette Culhane? Yes. Yes, she gloried, as his fingers undid the buttons of her blouse, his lips quick to take prisoner every inch of skin that was exposed by his efforts. She pulled his head down further, her breasts hard and aching, urgently calling for the warmth of his mouth.

Suddenly he stopped. Her eyes flew open in surprise. What she saw was a man fraught with desire. He scooped her into his arms. He was taking her into his bedroom, she thought. She hoped. She wrapped her arms about his neck, anticipation tingling in every part of her body as she curled against his hard chest.

Lovingly, as if she were a fragile doll, he laid her down on his bed. Within a moment he was next to her. She saw a slight pulsating motion in his throat that matched her own pulsebeat.

"Sit up for a second," he instructed, his voice deep

and husky, strained by the force of the passion she could feel emitting from him.

She did as she was told, and he took her jacket. Heat forged through her as he tossed it aside and pulled her toward him on the bed, his fingers resuming the task of freeing her from the confines of her blouse. Her nipples peaked harder still as he loosened the blouse from her shoulders.

"Kiss them, please," she whispered hoarsely. Her breathing almost choked her as each gasp of air struggled toward the surface; she was living for his next move. His mouth rained kisses over the upper planes of her breastbone, a zig-zag pattern of flame forming until his tongue lightly flicked over the filmy beige material of the lacy bra that lay between her and ecstasy. His mouth covered the tender expanse of her nipple, gently sucking it in, creating havoc within her.

Cully arched her back, urging the other breast toward him. Brandon complied, the ragged sound of his breath meshing with her own.

"Come to me, Evie; come to me," he rasped huskily against her skin, expertly unhooking the clasp of her bra and slipping the shred of material away. Cully thought her heart would burst as he kissed her heaving breasts once more, his tongue both teasing and enflaming, playful yet fiercely urgent.

And then his lips found hers again, quenching the almost bottomless thirst that waited there for him. His hot hands roamed the contours of her body, unfastening her skirt and slipping it away from her, then laying claim to everything he found there.

Before she fully realized it, she was nude, save for her delicate lace panties. And then he was there, too, his exploring hands ever so slowly slipping under the waistband, making the muscles of her stomach quiver involuntarily.

"I want to know every lovely inch of you," she heard him say somewhere in the mists that swirled about her head. And as the fabric moved lower and lower she felt the intricate pattern of his kisses move with it until she thought she would scream.

Cully suppressed a cry as the exquisite rapture seized her. Never had she known anything like this, never in her life had lovemaking been so gentle, so patient, involving every nerve ending she possessed.

"Get to know me too, Evie," his deep voice urged. The lightness of his tone, which she had come to know so well, was gone. In its place was the voice of a lover desiring to belong, to be loved. He led her hands to his own heaving chest, placing her fingertips on the buttons of his shirt. Quickly she opened them, her eyes never leaving the bittersweet look of passion on his face.

She stripped away his shirt, revealing the rippling muscles of his shoulders, the light, downy hair that feathered out across his perfect chest. She wanted to bury her face against it, to feel the light hairs tickle her cheek. She wanted him to belong to her as much as she did to him.

The shirt fell away to land in a crumpled heap on the side of the bed, and silently Brandon brought her hand to his belt buckle. The action was clear.

"I can't," she murmured, her eyes hooded by her lids. "I never . . ." She moved her hand away.

"Yes, you can," the seductive voice urged as he brought her hand back. "Yes, you can."

With trembling fingers she unbuckled the belt, then released the button that held the trousers over his taut stomach. The zipper slid down. She had never thought the sound of a zipper could excite her so. He moved slightly from side to side, aiding her work and shedding the trousers from his slim hips.

"You're not done," he rasped.

She barely heard the words as he guided her gently through the rest of her task. She almost gasped at the boldness that met her there. A small, agonizing, pleasure-filled moan escaped from Brandon's lips.

And then they were melting into one another, fusing their souls and their bodies as a spiral of overwhelming ardor caught them and lifted them to the highest plateau that could be scaled by two people. Cully thought she screamed his name, but the word was barely a whisper murmured against his ear as peace and exhaustion mingled freely through her limbs and her soul.

When she opened her eyes after her descent back to earth, Cully found him observing her, his deep blue eyes twinkling above her, a mixture of affection and mischief in them. "God, you were beautiful," he told her, nipping at her ear.

Despite her drained state, his action sent a tiny twinge of electricity through her. "You were no slouch yourself," she whispered back, still breathless.

Brandon chuckled, propping himself up further on his elbow. "Are you always so free with your compliments?" he asked teasingly, his hand almost absently tracing designs on her stomach.

Cully reached for the deep brown comforter that extended beneath her, meaning to throw the edge of it over her nude body. But he caught her hand.

"I'm very slow at completing my inventory," he told

her, the lightness of his tone laced with the desire that still smoldered there.

"I've never been studied under a microscope before," she said, turning her head away. Now that their passion had been met, a slight wave of embarrassment was overtaking her.

But Brandon turned her head back so that her eyes met his once again. "Then no one's ever appreciated you before," he told her, bringing his mouth back down on hers.

Time slipped away in a mist of ecstasy.

Cully could scarcely meet Madge's inquisitive gaze when she let herself into her apartment at three o'clock that morning. The woman had obviously been asleep on the loveseat. A bright test pattern was shining from the unattended television set.

"How was it?" Madge asked sleepily, rubbing her eyes and stretching before she rose. When she did, her eyes looked almost alert, searching Cully's face for clues.

"Fine," Cully said evasively. Fine? It had been exquisite.

A knowing grin filtered across Madge's round face, and she patted Cully's hand. "Terrific," she pronounced, heading for the door. "Terrific."

But was it so terrific? Cully wondered the next day as she gathered depositions from prospective character witnesses who were to appear at the Woolsey trial. Wouldn't the way she felt about Brandon hamper her usual competent manner in court? Dick had called her more of a man than he was when he had slammed the door on their life together. How would Brandon feel about her if she won the case? Would he be threatened? Would his masculinity suffer? Nagging doubts gnawed at her as she went about the business of putting a tighter case together.

Cully didn't go out to lunch, sending out for a sandwich instead. She tried to bury herself in her work so as not to think about her personal life. But the phone rang at three, and June wasn't around to take the call, having stepped away from her desk.

"Ms. Culhane," Cully said, propping the phone against her neck as she juggled some papers.

"Hi, gorgeous. Can I interest you in a cup of coffee after work?"

The sensual voice brought every vivid moment from the previous night back to her. The papers dropped from her hands. "You could interest me in buying a half share in the Brooklyn Bridge," she answered, a smile taking over her entire being.

"Sorry, out of luck," he told her. "I just sold the last share. Would you settle for half interest in me?" he posed.

"Only half?" she asked playfully.

"We could negotiate for the other half," he offered.

"Coffee will be fine," she laughed.

"You're an easy woman, Evie." His deep laugh brought warm waves to caress each part of her. "I'll meet you in the coffee shop down the block from your office at five," he told her.

"No," she said suddenly. "Someone might—"

"—see us?" he ended. "Okay. How about if we meet at Bristol's?"

What was she afraid of? she asked herself. Why was she skulking around like a kid? She wasn't doing anything unethical. So what if someone saw them together after work? They weren't discussing the case. "I've changed my mind," she told him.

"About me?"

"About meeting you at the coffee shop."

"Whew, you had me worried there," he teased. "See you at five, lover."

She hung up. Lover. Was she his lover? Was this the beginning of something, or just an interlude? And was she as "easy" as he had teased? Did his plans ultimately involve winning his case in the bedroom? It certainly would be a nice fringe benefit for him.

Cully's head began to ache.

After work Cully briskly left her office and hurried to the coffee shop on the corner. There was nothing wrong in them meeting like this, she told herself again. After all, she was an adult. She could handle all these brand new emotions that were exploding within her; she could put them in their proper place. She wasn't some wide-eyed teenager to let the rosy fingers of budding love color every aspect of her life. There was a clear line that separated how she felt about Brandon and how she felt about her case. At least she hoped that line was clear, she thought as she pulled the glass door of the coffee shop open and scanned the booths.

A warm feeling filled her as she saw the familiar dark head nod in her direction. He was already there, waiting for her in a tiny booth near the door. She walked over quickly, and he half rose in his seat as she joined him.

"If this is too close to the door for you . . ." he began, indicating his willingness to change booths.

But Cully shook her head, determined to stick to her principles. As long as she believed in herself, what other people might think didn't concern her. "This is fine," she told him, sliding in opposite him.

"I've missed you," he said, his eyes caressing her.

She laughed, hardly believing him but loving the way it sounded nonetheless. "It's only been half a day."

He glanced at his watch. "Fourteen hours and seventeen minutes to be exact," he told her.

A waitress came up, pencil poised, eyes darting appreciatively over Brandon. Cully doubted if the woman even took notice of her.

"Two coffees, please." Brandon glanced Cully's way. "Anything else?"

But she declined the desserts that beckoned to her from the menu. "No, thank you." She waited until the waitress had disappeared behind the counter. "You certainly are good for a woman's ego," she told him.

He smiled. It was a deep, all-embracing smile, and Cully longed to reach out and run her fingers over the sensual outline of his lips. "Good," he pronounced. "Does that mean you'll keep me around for a while?" he asked, taking her hand across the small table. She felt his forefinger run along the inside of her palm. Even that small action seemed intimate when he did it.

"Provided your other lady friends will let you out of their sight," she said coyly. The words surprised her. But then, she seemed to be full of surprises of late. Coyness wasn't part of her makeup. Neither was passion, she would have thought.

"I have no other lady friends," Brandon informed her, drawing his face into a serious expression. The very act looked playful.

"And I'm the Queen of Sheba," Cully replied with a

tolerant smile just as the waitress returned with their coffees.

"Glad to meet you, Your Highness," Brandon murmured. "Milk? Sugar?" he offered, pushing the items toward her.

She picked up the metal dispenser and poured a tiny stream of milk into her steaming black coffee, watching the white swirls mingle with the dark liquid until it reached the proper cocoa color.

"I asked you down here for a reason," Brandon said after a pause.

She lifted her eyes, ready for almost anything, steeling herself for the worst. "What?"

"I'd like to ask your permission to take Tim out this Saturday," he said.

A great wave of relief flooded through her. "Sure," she responded. "Where do you intend on whisking my son off to?" she asked.

"I thought we could start out with some skeet shooting—" Brandon began, taking a sip of his coffee.

"Skeet shooting?" she echoed. Somehow, she couldn't picture him shooting down little clay targets.

But he seemed quite enthusiastic about the subject, leaning over the table toward her as he spoke. "Sure. It's a lot of fun, helps build eye-hand coordination." Well, that explained his dexterity, she thought, amused. "And I figure it never hurts to get as much knowledge about everything as you can. You never know when it might come in handy."

"Right. You never know when you're going to be attacked by little clay pigeons and have to defend yourself," she said drolly.

"Do you have anything against skeet shooting?" he asked, mischievously baiting her.

"No, although it might be a little fairer if the skeet was armed, too," she said, knowing that she was talking nonsense and loving the totally relaxed feeling that enabled her to do so.

Brandon smiled, as if enjoying the sight of her being so buoyant. "How about coming along with us? You could be on the side of the skeet."

"Well . . ." she hedged. Already her mind was saying yes, but she wanted to be coaxed just a little.

"If I throw in an amusement park and dinner?" he offered.

She extended her hand to him. "You've got yourself a deal," she said.

"I hope so," Brandon said ever so softly.

Cully couldn't help wondering just what he meant by those words.

But Cully pushed all her uncertainties to the background on Saturday, rising extra early so that she could take a leisurely bath. She took a long time getting ready, choosing just the right outfit to look casual in. She had spent less time preparing some of her briefs, she thought. Just how much did this man mean to her?

A lot, she admitted to herself, running a thickly bristled hairbrush through the platinum waves of her shoulder-length hair. She had washed it and let it dry on its own. It now curled and tumbled about her face, and she looked a little like a blond gypsy in search of someone whose fortune she could tell.

What was her own fortune? she asked the reflection in the mirror, holding her brush in midair. No, don't explore this, she cautioned herself. Just enjoy the moment. *Forever* was too deep a word to contemplate, and fraught with possibilities for disappointment and heartache. She was just going to enjoy a fun-filled afternoon with her son and a man who excited her beyond belief. Tomorrow was something she would face tomorrow.

"Mom, how long are you going to take?" Timmy's voice rose impatiently outside her bedroom door. "He's gonna be here any minute."

"I'm almost ready," she called back, anchoring the hair near her left temple with a pretty hair clip of blue and white. It matched her outfit. She had settled on a peasant dress made up of three tiers of complementary shades of blue. The cream-colored top of her dress was gauzelike and adhered flatteringly to her trim, high breasts. She pulled the elastic neckline down until it rested enticingly on her alabaster shoulders, letting her thick hair curl against the bared skin. She took a light blue fringed shawl with her.

"Not bad, Cully, not bad," she declared happily, surveying the total picture.

That was obviously Brandon's opinion, too, as his eyes swept over her form quickly some ten minutes later. He bent his head and gave her a sweet, fleeting kiss that barely brushed against her willing lips.

"Hi, gorgeous," he said, then looked at Timmy's eager face. "Ready, Tiger?" he asked.

"He's been ready since last night, I think," Cully laughed.

"Well then, let's get going," Brandon urged, ushering them out.

Timmy ran ahead to the elevator.

"You look too gorgeous," Brandon breathed into

her ear, his warm breath sending messages all through her body. "I'm not sure I can keep my hands off you, especially with that neckline," he emphasized. And then he eyed her. "Is this some kind of test?" he asked suspiciously, his eyes sparkling. "Because if it is, you're arousing my manhood something awful."

"Shh," she chided, nodding her head toward Timmy, who turned around to face them at that moment.

"It's here!" he announced, pulling open the outside elevator door.

Brandon helped him with it. "It certainly is," Brandon said, his voice pregnant with a meaning that Cully wasn't sure she fathomed.

She couldn't remember a day she had enjoyed as much. This was what it could have been like if Dick had stayed, she thought, watching Brandon show Timmy how to hold a rifle. No, Dick had never had this kind of patience. He would never have made the kind of father that Brandon apparently could. She found herself wondering if Brandon would ever become a father. The role, surprisingly enough, seemed to fit him so well. He didn't talk down to Timmy. Rather, he treated him like an equal and explained everything the boy wanted to know.

"He's crazy about you," Cully told Brandon as she stood next to him, watching Timmy concentrate on getting the target within his sights.

Brandon slipped a protective hand onto the back of her neck. It felt so terribly right. "I'm crazy about him," he said. "You should be very proud of him," he added, watching Timmy. The clay pigeon fell to earth unharmed. ". . . even if he is a lousy shot," he muttered under his breath with a laugh.

The slope of Timmy's shoulders testified to his vast disappointment.

"Nice try," Brandon called out encouragingly, letting go of Cully and concerning himself with her son. "Hey," he said, looking down into the disappointed face, "it took me six months before the clay pigeons would stop laughing at me every time I walked out on the field," he told the boy. "Your form's a lot better than mine was when I started."

"Really?" Timmy asked, brightening.

"Sure, Tiger. Don't you worry. A few more sessions and you'll knock 'em dead," he promised.

"You think so?" Timmy asked.

"I know so," Brandon assured him. "I don't know about you two, but I sure could use a pizza," he said, smacking his lips hungrily.

"Me too," Timmy said solemnly, imitating Brandon's movements.

"Me three," Cully chimed in.

"Then it's unanimous," Brandon said, putting an arm about each of them. "Onward to the pizzeria!"

The rest of the afternoon went the same way. They shared everything. During their trip to the amusement park, all three rode the merry-go-round with its weather-beaten ponies. Brandon stretched, managing to secure the brass ring. Cully held her breath, afraid that he would lose his balance and fall. But he didn't. And he presented the ring to her when the ride ended.

Rather than use it for another ride, Cully tucked it away in her purse as a keepsake, telling herself that she was being silly all the while she was doing it.

Brandon watched her, seeming to understand her gesture. Still he teased, "You just want me to spend all my money," he said.

"Right you are," she laughed.

On the huge roller coaster, Brandon managed to squeeze in next to Cully, even though Timmy sat on her other side. He gave her a knowing look as their bodies pressed together. She made no effort to hide her smile.

As the exhilarating feeling of plummeting down the tall incline hit the pit of Cully's stomach, she dug her fingers into Brandon's arm. In a strange way she recognized the sensation as being akin to the one she had experienced when he had made love to her. Timmy's excited laughter filled the air, but she hardly heard it.

"Remind me never to Indian wrestle with you," Brandon laughed when they came to a halt. She had dug her nails in so hard that she had scratched his arm.

"Oh, did I do that?" she asked, embarrassed.

He nodded, then lowered his head so that only she could hear. "I'd rather have scratches like that on my back."

Cully felt a blush rising as she turned her head, hearing Brandon's chuckle in her ear.

They were almost too exhausted to eat, but Timmy seemed to come alive when Brandon brought them to a restaurant that boasted a multitude of video games in the back room. The boy hardly sat still long enough to finish his hamburger and french fries.

"Can I go now, Mom, can I?" he asked eagerly.

"It's 'may I,'" she corrected. "And yes, you may." She reached for her small shoulder bag, but Brandon was already handing Timmy a fistful of change.

"Today's on me, remember?" he reminded her.

Timmy ran off to the land of blinking lights and pinging noises, leaving Cully to revel in the light of Brandon's eyes.

"Today's really been wonderful for him," she told him, sipping her soda through a striped straw. "Thank you."

"My pleasure," Brandon said. "Speaking of pleasure," he began, "I've got a little place tucked away in the woods. How about coming up with me next weekend?"

Cully pretended to be occupied with searching out the last drop of soda amid a mini-mountain of ice chips at the bottom of her glass. "I'm a mother, Brandon. I can't just go running off for a weekend in the woods with some man."

"Sure you can. And I'm not just some man, remember?" he asked, putting his finger beneath her chin and raising her eyes to meet his. "It'll be fun," he promised.

She was sure it would be. As a matter of fact, *fun* was a poor term for it. But Cully doubted the wisdom of doing something like that. She was beginning to sorely doubt her ability to maintain a separation between work and her personal life. Brandon seemed to bring everything together in a swirling haze.

"We'll see," she murmured, turning to watch Timmy as he fed quarters into a machine that dwarfed him.

She felt Brandon put his hand over hers. Apparently he had taken her vague words as a commitment, she thought uneasily.

10

All the following week, Cully fought her own internal war. She wanted to go away with Brandon, and it was no longer his influence she feared. It was her own. She was falling in love with him—no, she *was* in love with him; there was no fooling herself. The more she was with him, the more she wanted to be with him, and the bigger a problem the pending trial became. She had to do her best, she told herself. She owed it to herself to be the best lawyer she could. And she owed it to Malcolm Woolsey.

Buried somewhere in all the legal terminology that boggled the ordinary mind were the old man's words: "Since Serena paid me no heed in life, I see no need for me to pay heed to her in death." It had been his way of striking back, of making up for the heartache Cully knew Serena had caused him. She couldn't let him down just because her own feelings were so confused.

But what a risk she ran, she thought miserably as she sat at her oak desk, rifling through her papers. To never see those eyes look at her again, smoldering with desire. To never feel those lips on her burning, parched skin . . .

"Snap out of it, Cully," she muttered to herself sternly. "You're a lawyer, not a lovesick adolescent. You can't let this affect your judgment about right and wrong."

It boiled down to that. If she sacrificed her principles for Brandon, she would feel like half a person. She wouldn't be able to face herself.

But could she face herself any easier if she sacrificed Brandon for her principles? It was a case of the lady or the tiger, and it made her terribly edgy.

"I'm telling you, you need a little vacation," Brandon urged her over the phone on Friday. He had called her every day, trying to persuade her to go away with him. Each time she heard his voice, all her well-chosen words of refusal melted in her throat and she had to struggle to bring them back to the surface.

Cully watched the four o'clock sun splash dazzling colors through her windowpane, casting a golden aura about the office. "It doesn't sound like I'd get much rest if we went up to your cabin," she said, playing with the phone cord, wrapping it and rewrapping it around her forefinger.

"We each have our own definition of *vacation*," he said huskily. "I like mine best. What do you say?" he asked. "Please?"

She could almost feel the ripples of his warm breath

on her skin as he uttered the single word in a low, purring growl.

She knew that she shouldn't go, that her final answer to him should be "no." But she heard herself answer almost as if she were another person. "All right."

"Terrific," he enthused. "Madge said she'd have no problem staying with Tim."

"You talked to Madge?" she asked, surprised. Was there no end to his self-confidence?

"I don't leave things to chance," he informed her lightly.

No, he didn't. She knew that much about him. He had probably orchestrated her falling in love with him as well. But it was too late to have second thoughts about that—much too late. Already she could feel her body tensing with anticipation as she thought of the coming weekend.

"I'll give you three hours to get ready," he told her. "And then I'm coming to get you."

"But I haven't packed yet," she protested.

"Good," he said. "The less you bring, the less there'll be to get in the way. Oh, and Evie—"

"Yes?"

"I sleep in the raw."

The image lit a fire in her very core. She tried to keep her voice steady. "Oh? Doesn't it get cold up there?"

"I plan to light my own fire," he told her. "See you in three hours."

Cully was left with a phone in her hands and a strange tightness in the pit of her stomach.

* * *

She shouldn't be doing this, she told herself, tossing things into her suitcase. She should get on that phone, call Brandon and call the weekend off. People just didn't go away with a man for the weekend. At least, she didn't. But this wasn't just some man. This was *the* man, the man who made her very soul sing.

What tune would it be singing after next week? her mind asked. Next week was the trial.

"I'll handle next week when it comes, she told herself firmly. She was getting tired of all these internal arguments. They never led anywhere.

She snapped the lid of her powder blue suitcase shut, absently wondering if she had covered all bases with her packing. She wasn't thinking too clearly. How about next Tuesday? How clearly would she be thinking then? Would she sit beside Randolph and Andrea remembering only how it felt to be enveloped in Brandon's arms? She shouldn't go. She shouldn't run the risk of muddling her mind further . . .

No, she had to have faith in herself. She had done everything legally and humanly possible to block whatever argument Brandon might bring to bear concerning the case. She was prepared. She had all the evidence, the testimony—all the cards. The rest was up to the judge and the jury. She was free to enjoy herself, perhaps for the last time, she added sadly, brushing away the wisps of hair that fell naturally at her temple as she gave her appearance a last once-over.

When the doorbell rang, she squared her shoulders. "Into the valley of death rode the six hundred," she muttered, recalling a line from Tennyson.

But it was the valley of pleasure she was hoping for.

Cully cast one last apprehensive eye toward Timmy as Brandon picked up her suitcase. Madge swept up to the boy's side, putting her arm about his shoulders.

"Don't give it another thought," she said, as if reading the uncertainty in Cully's eyes. "Everything's going to be great on this end. Timmy and I are going to go to the movies, eat food you don't approve of and stay up late, right, Timmy?" the older woman asked, fondly tousling the boy's blond hair.

The grin on Timmy's face set all of Cully's fears to rest. Now all she had to worry about was herself.

The drive up to Brandon's cabin was made more spectacular by the colorful, fading rays of the setting sun, which played hide and seek with them through the trees as they drove along the narrow two-lane road. The azure sky melted into purple before it finally allowed itself to be cloaked in a star-studded black. Seductive music flowed from the car's tape deck. A feeling of peace slowly took hold of Cully and she sighed.

"How much farther is it?" she asked. Nothing but dark shadows cast by the trees on either side of them broke across the steady path of the winding road.

"Can't wait either, eh?" Brandon asked.

"My leg's got a cramp in it," she told him, pretending to be evasive.

"Mine too," he said significantly, planting a quick kiss on her cheek.

Cully pressed her lips together in secret delight.

She had expected a little cabin nestled picturesquely in the woods and had hoped that it would have indoor plumbing. She was definitely not prepared for what she saw.

"It's like a chalet," she said, looking at the cement steps that led up to the front door. The cabin was perched on a hill, and behind it was a magnificent view of a man-made lake. It almost seemed silly that this region of a thousand lakes needed to have one more imposed by man's own hand. But she had to admit later, when she saw it by dawn's first light, that it was breathtaking no matter how it had gotten there.

"What, this old thing?" Brandon teased, following her inside with their suitcases. "I picked it up for a song."

"Must have been a whole musical," she said, marveling as she looked around. The huge living room, with its beamed, vaulted ceiling, was wrapped about a beautiful, two-sided white brick fireplace that beckoned invitingly in the moonlight.

Brandon flipped on a switch and a dim, romantic light permeated the room, enabling Cully to scan the area better.

"The kitchen is off to the right," Brandon told her. "And the little girls' room is off to the back," he pointed out for her.

"I'm not a little girl," she corrected him playfully, still looking around.

He wrapped his arms about her waist from behind, hugging her close. "Yes, I know," he murmured, nibbling on her ear, his tongue outlining it with quick, darting motions.

Already she felt herself dissolving into him, and she hadn't even taken off her suede jacket.

"And my room?" she asked innocently, trying to keep her breath steady.

"*Our* room is off to the left," he told her, still not letting go.

"Only one bedroom?" she asked, turning around. "I'm surprised. It looks like such a big cabin, too."

In reply, Brandon laughed and picked her up in his arms, lifting her as if she weighed nothing at all. "Lady, if you think I brought you all the way up here just to have separate quarters, you're not as sharp as I gave you credit for." He nuzzled her, then covered her lips with short, teasing kisses that ended before she could get utterly lost in them.

"Are you hungry?" he wanted to know.

"Yes," she answered.

"Good, so am I," he told her and proceeded to carry her into the bedroom.

"I meant for food," she said, laughing, stopping his entrance into the room by putting her smartly booted foot up against the doorway.

"Food for the soul . . ." he murmured, kissing the side of her neck.

". . . comes after food for the stomach," she ended. "You can't make love to a woman whose stomach is growling."

"Try me," he challenged, his eyes bright. "But," he sighed, putting her down, "in the interests of being a gentleman, I'll bring in the basket."

"Basket?" she asked, unbuttoning her jacket to expose a bright pink blouse that was held together with only three buttons.

"I packed a picnic dinner," he told her over his shoulder as he headed out to his car.

"The man thinks of everything," she marveled out loud in teasing admiration.

"Always," he shot back as he disappeared into the darkness.

Always, she thought, chewing on her lip.

By the time he got back, Cully was working on getting a fire started. Brandon hunched down next to her, shaking his head in amazement. "I didn't know city girls knew how to start fires—at least, not ones that require real logs."

"I was a Girl Scout," she informed him proudly. "We learned all sorts of useful things."

"Like how to fight off an ardent admirer?" he asked, arching his brow.

"That they didn't cover," she said glibly.

"Lucky me," he said just before he kissed her.

Her head was spinning and her senses flamed higher than the tiny sparks that flickered in the fireplace. But Brandon didn't push his advantage. Instead he released her and pushed the basket toward her.

"Cold chicken and wine," he said, sitting down and crossing his legs before him, Indian fashion.

"I see you have the proverbial bearskin rug by the fireplace," she noted, nodding at it as she made herself comfortable on the deep brown pile.

"Shot him myself when you said you'd come up here with me," he joked.

"Why?" she bantered back, accepting the cold drumstick he offered her. It tasted delicious. Everything was delicious!

"So I could roll your nude body up in it and then have the supreme pleasure of unwrapping it slowly, an exciting inch at a time."

He was doing it to her again, tantalizing her without even laying a hand on her. What power the man had. How easily he manipulated people's emotions, she thought. The image he painted for her was as vivid in her mind as if the scene had already taken place.

He grinned at her. "You've stopped eating," he

pointed out. She wondered if that was a hint of triumph flickering in his eyes.

Right then, she didn't care. She knew what was going to happen as well as he did. Excitement kissed every part of her flesh.

"I think my appetite's shifting," she murmured softly, mesmerized by the tender glow coming from his eyes. The firelight played off his face, bathing it in seductively golden hues.

Quietly Brandon took the forgotten chicken piece from her hand and carelessly dropped it back into the basket. Ever so slowly he licked the few remaining crumbs from her fingers, watching her face as he did so. Each pass of his tongue aroused her more. Her breath came in smaller and smaller snatches; she was waiting, anticipating.

"There are always so many buttons with you," he growled sensuously against her cheek, kissing the outline of her jaw as his swift, sure fingers undid her blouse and searched for the pliant softness that quivered beneath it.

His hands, so smooth, so gentle, explored the now familiar terrain of her breasts almost languidly as his lips drank in more and more of her offered sweetness. His kiss increased in fervor as he found more and more passion meeting him.

Cully wondered if he could feel the hammering of her heart beneath his hand. The pulsating rhythm seemed to control every part of her as Brandon's fingers spread their magic touch down toward the waistband of her jeans, flicking them open with ease and then sliding further down to take possession of what he found there—or to repossess what was already his alone.

She felt herself arching against him, wanting him to progress more quickly, yet reveling in each slow movement, as if a piece of heaven had been granted to her. Her own hands quickly opened his shirt so that she could feel the fleecy hairs of his chest rubbing against her hardening breasts. She wanted to soothe the aching that existed there, but her action only made things worse. It fired both the flame that burned within her and the one that rose within Brandon, because she heard a muffled moan that sounded like her name come from his lips.

Rocking her gently against him, Brandon laid her down on the rug they had been laughing about only minutes before. His hypnotic, sky blue eyes devoured her, showing her a mixture of tenderness and mounting desire. There was no mischief there, no hidden humor—only passion. Cully raised her arms and allowed him to free her completely from the blouse; then she entwined her hands about his neck, bringing his head down toward her.

She felt his first kiss before it actually touched her, her breath sharpening as his lips moved from hers to the sensual hollow of her throat, forging a path to her breasts, which moved against him demandingly. Finally, his hand cupped one, bringing it to his scorching mouth, caressing it with his lips until the bud was unspeakably hard.

Her whole being was a mass of contradictions, she thought distantly as she shuddered beneath his touch, her softness aware of the hardening demands of his body. His hair tickled her chin, and she was tempted to laugh just a little, a pleasure-laden laugh. But all that came from her throat was the deep sound of his name over and over.

She didn't really know when he removed the last shred of her clothing. It all seemed to melt off into the background. Nothing existed except for the two of them and their world that began and ended with the soft, furry rug. The cabin walls had drifted out into eternity.

The feel of the rug's fur mingled and blended with the feel of the hairs on Brandon's body, exciting her as they brushed against her ivory white skin.

"Oh, Evie, what a talent you have for reducing me to a primitive male," Brandon rasped against her mouth, his chest partially covering her as his hands still explored her lower half, caressing her, making her his over and over again. She was throbbingly aware of each tiny inch traveled by his fingers. Her flesh fairly danced as he progressed up the sensitive area of her inner thigh until his hand came to rest on the most private spot of all. But he didn't stop for long. His massaging hand passed over it again and again.

"Now, Brandon, now," she groaned.

But in reply she felt the grasp of his hand upon hers, leading her to him. The unspoken message was as clear as if he had uttered each word. With haste, her heart beating in her ears, Cully opened his belt, then parted the material beneath, fumbling, yet with a sureness driven by deep need.

There. He was just as naked as she. The thought rang triumphantly through her for a scant second. And then there were no more thoughts, nothing but flourishing ecstasy that grew and grew as Brandon covered her body with his own.

His tongue invaded the sweet entrance of her mouth at the same time as she parted her legs, admitting him. There was no room to even pull in her breath. Her eager hands held him closer, ever closer, and they merged their bodies as a melody composed in the heavens took over. They moved as one, toward one mutual goal . . . toward one mutual paradise.

The crackle of the flames in the fireplace could not begin to match the snap of electricity she felt within her as they made love.

"Not bad for openers," Brandon whispered against her hair as they lay before the fireplace some time later, her body cupped familiarly against his own, as if it were another part of the whole.

"Openers?" Cully marveled in exhaustion. "What do you mean, 'openers'?"

Brandon propped himself up on his elbow, his powerful body set aglow by the fire's light. Cully couldn't keep her eyes off him. Every inch of his body was muscular and made with perfection in mind. Just the very sight of it did things to her pulse that nothing else ever had, ever could.

"Lady," Brandon promised in a low voice as his forefinger sensuously traced the outline of her lips, "you ain't seen nothin' yet."

With that he playfully gathered her up in the bearskin rug, then rose with his bundle.

"What are you doing?" she asked, putting her arm around his neck to steady herself.

"I'm a man of my word," he told her, carrying her off to the bedroom.

Cully saw the look of desire rekindling in Brandon's eyes as he set her down on the bed. "You're a man of iron," she quipped as a tingly, delicious anticipation began to throb through her body once again. "Aren't you tired?" she asked.

Brandon kept the rug about her body as he sat down next to her. "Tired is for bored old men playing solitaire. I've got something far more enticing than a deck of cards to hold in my hands," he told her, slowly unwrapping her, pulling the soft fur away from her body a tantalizing inch at a time, just as he had fantasized about doing earlier. He was stroking her with it. Cully bit her lip to keep a moan of ecstasy from escaping as the fur slid away from her breasts.

"Part one," Brandon murmured, his fingers working their way down, slipping the fur from her middle. Her taut belly quivered. "Part two." Cully could hardly contain herself. First came the stroking sensation of the fur as it moved away from her thighs, then came the sensuous touch of his warm breath upon them as he uttered thickly, "Part three. The unveiling is over." With that Brandon moved to kiss her, claiming the area that the bearskin rug had covered only moments before. Cully gave herself up to the rapture.

"C'mon, you gonna sleep all day?"

The words roused Cully from the light sleep she had fallen into. She opened her eyes, and the first thing she saw was Brandon looming over her. She reached up for him.

"Oh, no, I'm not falling into your tender trap," he teased, moving back in the bed.

"*My* tender trap?" she cried, sitting up. The bright blue sheet fell away from her breasts, exposing their fullness. His eyes took full advantage of the situation. "You were the one—" she began.

"Lies, all lies. You lured me up here, then took

advantage of my innocence," he said, sitting down on the bed, still magnificently nude, still tempting her.

"Innocence?" she scoffed. "You don't know the meaning of the word."

"Maybe not," he said, "but I know the meaning of the word *lust*," he told her, moving in closer.

"Lust? Is that all this is?" she asked, her voice still playful, but tinged with a bit of doubt.

"That, and a whole lot more—a whole lot more," he murmured just before he took what had been preordained as his.

They spent a wonderful day together. At least, it started out as wonderful. Cully loved the peacefulness of the area, and they had an idyllic time, laughing and loving, partaking of the simple things that Brandon had seen fit to bring. For lunch he took her into the small town that she was surprised to find existed not too far away from his hideaway.

He came to a stop before a rustic-looking emporium that seemed to have been fashioned a hundred years earlier. The rest of the town consisted of a few shops and half a dozen houses. The emporium met all the main needs. It doubled as a post office and a grocery store handling the main staples of life, such as coffee.

"Can't live without coffee," Brandon told her, buying a can of one of the more popular brands. "How about two cups here?" he asked the middle-aged man behind the counter.

The man peered over his rimless glasses, looking Cully over carefully before he ventured an approving smile. "Sure thing," he said. He disappeared, but soon reemerged with two steaming cups of black liquid.

Cully and Brandon drank them while sitting on barrels that served as stools arranged around a rough table. They shared the space with an opened, half-filled crate of canned baby peas. Cully couldn't remember when she had sampled coffee that had made her feel so alive.

Later Brandon took her fishing for their dinner.

"But it's a man-made lake," she protested, standing on the bank and holding the fishing pole Brandon had produced for her out of the recesses of one of his closets.

"So?" he asked, casting out his line expertly.

"What are we going to catch?" she teased. "Man-made fish?"

"No, silly, the lake is well stocked. I made sure before I bought the place," he told her, sitting down and resting his plaid-shirted back against a weeping willow.

It all looked rather hopeless to her. "What if we don't catch anything?" she prodded.

"Then they'll find us starved to death, wrapped in each other's arms, naked, with huge smiles on our faces." He grinned at the image.

"You're crazy," she laughed, shaking her head as she cast her line out next to his and sat down beside him.

"Like a fox," he told her. "Look who I picked to starve with."

She felt an inner glow burning all through her.

11

But Cully's inner glow dimmed slightly as they talked.

"Evie?"

"Hmm?"

"Why did you become a lawyer?" he asked casually.

She turned toward him, wondering what had prompted the question, but his normally expressive countenance gave her no clue. He just stared straight ahead, appearing mesmerized by the tranquility of the scene before him.

"There was never anything else I wanted to do," she finally answered.

"I'm surprised you didn't go into criminal law, what with your zeal," he teased slightly.

"I thought of that," she confessed. "And maybe I will, someday. But there's a lot to be said for our line of work. I'm helping people put their lives in order. Granted, it's not as exciting as criminal work, but it has its own rewards." The laugh felt a little dry in her throat as she uttered it. The subject was getting too serious. Was he going to try to influence her? she wondered. Oh, please, don't spoil it, her mind pleaded with him.

Behind him, the sun was disappearing into the lake, its reflected light twice as bright as the original. But Cully didn't see the sun or its beauty as she watched Brandon's profile intently.

"Oh, it has its excitement," he assured her quietly. ". . . and its traumas," he added after a pause.

"Traumas?" Despite herself, she couldn't help echoing the word in confusion.

"Being cut out of a will can be a traumatic experience."

Her mouth hardened slightly. "Especially to Serena's pocketbook," she said wryly. Was this what the weekend was about after all?

"I wasn't particularly speaking about Serena," he said, still looking at the sparkling water. The rays of the sun rippled colorfully toward shore, but the peacefulness was gone for Cully.

She remembered, as she heard Brandon's words, that he had mentioned being cut out of his father's will. Perhaps this case represented something more than just a nice percentage of the winnings to him. Perhaps he was fighting for his own set of principles, she thought unhappily. That was going to make Tuesday and the days that followed all the more unbearable.

"If you want to talk about traumas," she heard herself saying, her voice not as soft as before, "how about the trauma of being cut out of someone's life?"

"What?" It was his turn to be puzzled.

"I saw an old man waiting to hear from his daughter on his birthday, an old man who knew he might not live to see another birthday—as he didn't," she said quietly. "I saw the hurt look in his eyes while he tried to cover his wounds with gruff words. He didn't deserve that kind of treatment. There was no excuse for it."

The air hung above them, still, except for the cry of a faraway bird that drifted across the sky.

"Well," Brandon said finally, rising. "I guess we both know where we stand." He extended his hand toward her. She took it, allowing him to help her up.

"Yes, I guess we do," she replied a bit solemnly.

Then a grin cracked his face. "No reason why we can't still be bosom buddies," he told her playfully, slipping his arm about her shoulders.

But there was, Cully thought miserably. There was a reason why they couldn't stay the way they were. The case sounded as if it meant as much to him as it did to her.

"C'mon," he urged. "Don't look so sad. I didn't mean it when I said we'd starve. I packed some extra chicken," he told her, taking up her rod as well as his own.

"Chicken again?" she groaned, relieved that she had something to hide behind. But her heart felt heavy.

"I thought you loved my chicken," he protested as he led her back to his cabin.

* * *

But it wasn't his chicken she loved, she thought very early the next morning as she rose silently, taking care to be quiet as she gathered up her clothes. It was him, and if she stayed with him any longer, all her principles would dissolve in the heat of her passion. She wouldn't be able to live with herself if that happened.

Cully dressed quickly in the dark, then stole out into the living room, casting one long backward glance at Brandon before she left. He looked almost like an innocent boy, his dark hair touseled and falling into his eyes. Cully closed the door softly as she felt tears coming to her eyes.

She found some paper in a kitchen drawer and hastily wrote him a note, feeling that he needed some sort of explanation for her flight. But how could she ever put all her feelings down on paper? The end result didn't meet with her satisfaction, but she couldn't afford to waste time. He would be up and looking for her any moment. Once again, she scanned the short note.

Dear Brandon,

I love you. I think a smart lawyer like you has probably figured that out by now. But I still intend to fight you all the way on this. I believe in the case. My clients deserve a good lawyer, and I intend to be one. I can't just let you win, no matter what my heart tells me to do.

She had gone on to sign it "Cully," then scratched it out and wrote "Evie." That was who she was when she was with him—not proud, competent, self-assured Cully, but Evie, a warm woman who could love once again. That was the heart of the problem.

After putting the note down where Brandon would find it, Cully picked up her suitcase and swiftly made her way back into the little town where she and Brandon had had such fun just the day before. After knocking persistently, she managed to rouse both the owner of the emporium and his wife, who eyed her curiously. It took a lot of convincing on Cully's part, but finally the owner reluctantly agreed to drive her back to Chicago.

Cully had made good her escape, at least physically. Mentally was another story.

When she let herself into her apartment later that morning, Timmy was already up, and he began bombarding her with questions she didn't feel up to answering. Even worse were the obvious questions in Madge's eyes.

"Was it fun, Mom?" Timmy wanted to know as she brought her suitcase into her room.

"Yes," she said, trying to smile down at his eager face. "It was fun."

"Is he going to be my new dad?" Timmy blurted out, not knowing how much his words hurt her. "Is he, Mom?"

She wet her lips, recalling the strange sound in Brandon's voice when he had said that being cut out of a will was a traumatic experience. "I don't think so," she said quietly.

"Aw, why, Mom?" Timmy asked, almost pleading. As if the choice were up to her, she thought ruefully.

Well, maybe the choice was up to her, she thought later after Madge had volunteered to take Timmy to yet another movie, leaving Cully to pull herself together in peace. But the price tag was too high. Much too high.

Even when Dick had walked out on her, she hadn't felt this awful aching, this bewildering emptiness. Cully couldn't sit in one place for more than a minute, so she wandered about her apartment. Even a vigorous workout at her health club didn't help relieve the nerve-wracking tension that she was feeling.

Brandon didn't call. Not that night, nor on Monday. Her phone at the office was far from still, and each time it rang her heart jumped. But it wasn't Brandon. It was always someone else, someone needing to know something, someone trying to make an appointment with her—never Brandon.

She walked into court on Tuesday, praying for the inner calm that had always seen her through before.

She found her way into the courtroom blocked by a tangle of news reporters and cameramen from the local television stations who needed something to fill their evening broadcasts with. A cacophony of voices assaulted her ears, forming half questions that were drowned out by other half questions. They all insisted on asking her things she wasn't allowed to answer and wouldn't have answered even if she could. It was a circus, she thought angrily, trying to hustle Andrea and Randolph away from the prying eyes of the cameras.

Suddenly the crowd shifted away from them. Brandon and Serena were on the scene. Serena had never looked lovelier. Cully was sure that Brandon had instructed the woman to forego her usual flamboyant clothing. Wearing a tasteful, flattering dress, she looked picture perfect.

As did he, Cully thought. Brandon, dressed in a light

gray, three-piece designer suit, was the definitive picture of the competent lawyer leading his client into the courtroom. Expertly, he fielded all the questions hurled at him, answering only where prudent, making sure to smile all the while.

Briefly his eyes met Cully's, but there was no nod of the head, no intimate, private gesture—not even a sign of recognition. He was out to win.

Well, so was she, she thought, squaring her shoulders and marching into the courtroom.

The fifteen rows of spectator seating were packed with people. She hardly saw any of them as she made her way to the table where she would sit with Andrea and Randolph.

"It's going to be fine," she assured them coolly, sitting down.

Was it? her heart demanded.

Cully looked over at the gaping emptiness of the two rows of the jury box. That was going to have to be filled, she thought, and filled well. How was she going to find enough people who were immune to Brandon's charm and who could see the case without the ribbons and the clever packaging that he was going to try to surround it with?

She was going to make them see it, she told herself, clenching her hands in her lap. She had to.

The rest of that day's session was spent in choosing the jury. Cully used every maneuver available to block Brandon's attempts to pack the box with sympathetic males. She implemented her ten peremptory challenges as judiciously as possible. But try as she might, she knew that her *voir dire*—the questioning of the jurors—was not as smooth as Brandon's. He was totally at ease, forming his questions as if he were talking to old friends in the comfort of his living room. . . . His living room, where they had begun to make love— No, stop it, her mind cried, desperately pulling her back to the tense atmosphere in the courtroom. Think of that later, later. For now he was an opponent to beat, nothing more.

Surely his manner was indicative that he felt that way. He acted as if he didn't know her. Her doubts surfaced again. Had everything that had happened between them been just a ruse to get her to this near-faltering state? Certainly his eyes held no warmth within them when he looked her way. It was all over. What she thought had existed between them had become a casualty of the duel that was now taking place. Cully mentally girded herself for the battle ahead.

By the middle of the next session, the jury had been selected. The jurors weren't all to Cully's liking, but she had to admit that she didn't feel as if the box was "packed" against her. She was holding her own.

Cully continued to hold her own in their opening statements to the jury. Brandon seemed to have the six men, six women in the palm of his hand, but Cully was sure that her words had at least vividly painted a picture of a hurt father. Gruff, to be sure, but hurt nonetheless.

It remained to be seen how the testimony would affect them.

Brandon brought out one witness after another who testified to Malcolm Woolsey's rather erratic behavior in the last few months of his life. They told how he would fire people for apparently no reason, how he would erupt suddenly in anger that seemed to have no basis. He would seclude himself for hours at a time, they said, alone except for his nurse, who hung on sheerly because it was her job.

Cully listened intently, making copious notes. Randolph had paid the nurse well for her services. Would Brandon now use the harsh-looking woman's words against them? she wondered, watching him as he rose to examine the witness.

Brandon deftly managed to get the nurse to admit that Woolsey was a most trying patient. He would sit and talk to himself, having no use for the people who surrounded him, delighting instead in verbally abusing them. Time and again, Randolph had been humiliated in his father's presence.

A clear picture was materializing as to why Serena totally avoided her father's presence. Brandon was creating the scenario ever so subtly, showing a picture of Randolph and Andrea coercing their mentally enfeebled parent to strike their older sister out of the will. After all, Brandon's manner seemed to indicate, they felt they had earned his money by putting up with him and suffering his berating words.

Day number two ended on that note, but those that followed were better. Cully felt that her witnesses conducted themselves well, and that the case was hers.

On the evening before the final day's testimony Cully went home, mentally and physically drained. In the morning she would put her key witness on the stand, Woolsey's long-time family physician, a man who had known him inside and out for thirty years. She played back in her mind her pretrial questioning of the man and decided that she had nothing to worry about, despite Brandon's obvious love affair with the jury.

It was only his love affair with her that was in jeopardy, her mind taunted her over and over. Never had she faced a possible victory with such foreboding and dread.

And the questions she didn't pose in her own mind, Madge put into words for her later that evening.

"It's going too well, isn't it?" the worried woman asked, sitting down on Cully's sofa. She had come in on the pretext of needing a little company, but they both knew she was there to ask well-meaning questions.

"What do you mean by that?" Cully asked, her hand on her forehead, massaging the front of her brow, which ached fiercely. She put her feet up, sans shoes, on an ottoman. Timmy, mercifully, was closeted in his room with some homework and his favorite records.

"You're going to win," Madge guessed. "The case, I mean."

"And that's 'going too well'?" Cully asked. Her laugh was hollow.

"You know what I mean," Madge said, her voice deadly serious.

Cully dropped her hand and looked at her aunt, studying the round, warm face quietly. "Are you telling me to throw the case?" she asked in a hushed voice.

Madge shrugged, apparently not wanting to use just those words. "No, not exactly." She hesitated for a moment, then went on. "Just don't try to win so hard. Look," she pleaded, reaching out and taking hold of Cully's forearm as if for emphasis, "the Woolseys have a lot of money. What does it matter if they divide it two ways or three ways? They can afford it. Can you afford to lose Brandon?" she pressed. Her hazel eyes searched Cully's face for an answer.

Cully sighed, tired of the dilemma, tired of trying to face that possibility. How many times had her ex-husband's words come back to haunt her in the past two days? "You're a better man than I, Evie."

"So you think I'll lose him if I win?" Cully asked quietly.

"Men are men, Evie. No matter what era we're in, they still don't like being shown up by a woman, especially *their* woman," Madge told her.

Cully rose, went over to the Oriental hutch and ran her fingers absently over the intricate carvings. It had been delivered the same day that Brandon had barged into her life. "What makes you think he sees me in that light? Maybe," she said, swinging back around, "maybe it was all a game to him, a tactic. Maybe he *was* trying to win this case in the bedroom, hoping that I would think and feel just the way you do right now."

But Madge shook her head firmly. "Not Brandon."

"He's not a saint, Madge," Cully said in irritation, fighting herself more than her aunt. She felt like a rat in a maze.

"No," the older woman agreed. "He's not. But he is a good man. He cares about you, Evie; I can see it in his eyes. And he cares about Timmy. What are you going to tell Timmy when Brandon doesn't come around anymore?"

"That he has a mother he can be proud of," Cully said with conviction, her fists clenched defensively at her sides.

"Can't he be proud of his mother for making a good choice of husband for a change?" Madge asked wearily.

But Cully shook her blond head firmly. "Not at the price you're asking me to pay."

Cully felt less firm the next morning in court. Brandon hadn't attempted to make any eye contact with her since that first day in the hall when their paths had been obstructed by television cameras and reporters. It was as if he were being charming to everyone but her. She was the enemy, and he wasn't wasting his time or charm on her, she thought ruefully.

Well, it wouldn't do him any good, she thought. The case was going to be hers.

Dr. Rose, a quiet, soft-spoken man, testified to his long acquaintance, both socially and professionally, with Malcolm Woolsey. Cully allowed him to use his own words to describe the effect that the robust man's physical deterioration had had on his behavior and emotions. She was sure she had the jury's sympathy for Woolsey's anguish at losing the use of his once powerful limbs. The disease had relegated a doer to the sidelines of life.

"One more thing, doctor, and I want you to think very, very carefully now. Could the Parkinson's disease have affected his mind in any manner so as to render him incompetent and unable to handle his own affairs—unable to draw his own conclusions?" Cully stressed significantly.

"Not in my opinion," the doctor told her. "He was as sane a man as anyone I have ever met," the old man answered firmly.

"Your witness," Cully said, stepping down.

Brandon, Cully saw, did try his best. He wasn't pulling any punches. Several times Cully was moved to object to his line of questioning; once she protested that he was trying to lead the witness. The judge sustained her objections each time, much to Cully's relief and partial surprise. No amount of clever verbal footwork shook the doctor's testimony. The best Brandon could do was to get the man to admit that in *some* cases the disease could affect the mind enough to diminish the patient's mental capacities.

Cully closed her eyes after the doctor stepped down. It was over. Everything but the summations. Since Brandon represented the plaintiff, he went first. His was a speech that called upon the jurors to see his client as a cast-off child, a child more sinned against than sinning. She was being made to pay for her rather high-spirited youth by vengeful younger siblings who could only yearn after the life that Serena had lived so fully. They had taken advantage of their father's weakened spirits, his depression over being deprived from living life to the fullest himself, and made him part of their jealousy. They had seen their triumph in the rewriting of the will.

Brandon sat down, content with the effect his words had had on the jury. Cully pressed her lips together. He had made it rough. She was aware of the fact that, despite the strength of her case, the jury responded better to him personally than to her. She was too removed, too cool. He was impassioned. So be it, she told herself, opening her jacket, mimicking the gesture Brandon had just used. She was determined to become one with the jury, just as he had.

"Ladies and gentlemen of the jury, my most worthy opponent would have you believe that my clients are devious, vengeful people, the sort you might find in a very poor melodrama. He would have you believe that the late Malcolm Woolsey was a feeble-minded old man, able to be manipulated. Yet all the testimony shows that even if his legs were useless, his mind was not. He exercised power to the very end, making the decisions that determined the course of his business empire. Of course he responded bombastically at times—wouldn't you if you were made to sit, when once you could run?" she asked, searching each one of the jurors' faces intently.

"Coming to grips with a debilitating disease is not easy, and one can forgive Mr. Woolsey if at times he acted bitterly, impatient with people who were far healthier in body than he was." She swung around, scanning their faces, her voice growing in volume. "But we are not talking about his body today. We are talking about his mind, and there was nothing wrong with that. It wasn't a cloudy brain that made him change his will, not whispered, coercive words. To Mr. Randolph Woolsey's own testified chagrin, his father never bothered to consult him about anything. Why would he suddenly listen to him about something so private, so personal, as his will?" she demanded. "No, what prompted Malcolm Woolsey to change his will was a broken heart—the broken heart of an abandoned, unheeded, unloved father. Serena Woolsey did not concern herself with her father's affairs or with her father. But now she is here, begging you to allow her to concern herself with her father's money."

Cully drew herself up to her full height, true anger blazing in her eyes. "A decision for the plaintiff would be unfair. Worse than that, it would be a crime against the heart."

With that, Cully sat down. Covertly she stole another glance, not at the jury this time, but at Brandon, wondering how he had reacted to this new side of her.

She had never sounded so full of passion before, had never actually pleaded with a jury before. Previously she had always laid down the facts, highlighting the important ones, and let them speak for themselves. This time she was trying, she admitted, to out-Brandon Brandon.

The jury rose as one and was led off to be sequestered. The judge banged his gavel. Court was in recess.

Cully hardly slept all night, tossing and turning, not knowing what to hope for. She was damned, she felt, in either case. She had done her very best to beat him, and although a verdict her way would add salt to Brandon's wounds, even if she lost he wasn't likely to forget the fact that she had tried to beat him. No, not for a very long time.

Madge and Timmy came to court the next day, Madge arguing that Timmy had a lot riding on the outcome of the trial. Cully couldn't bring herself to tell them that as far as her romance with Brandon was concerned, the end, she felt, was a foregone conclusion. She had read no inviting warmth in his eyes. There had been nothing but polite civility in his manner toward her.

Later that morning the jury foreman handed the jury's decision to the bailiff, who in turn handed it to the judge. Cully held her breath during the endless moments as the judge scanned the note. He banged his gavel for silence and cleared his throat.

"'We the jury,'" he read, "'decide in favor of the defense.'"

It was all over.

12

Cully wasn't sure just how she had managed to get back to her office. She remembered something about taking a cab, not having wanted to walk the short distance the way she usually did. She also vaguely remembered turning down Randolph's exuberant offer to go out and celebrate.

She knew she had tried to exchange a few words with Timmy and Madge. But nothing had sounded right, and she had left, trusting her aunt to take Timmy home. She would be there by and by, she had promised.

She had lied to them when she had said there were things she still had to see to at the office. Her calendar was empty for the day, since she hadn't been sure just how long the trial would go on. Now time hung heavily on her hands. The hearty congratulations she received at the office did nothing to raise her spirits.

"I knew old Brandon couldn't get the best of you, Eve," Abernathy had said proudly when she had returned.

Cully had barely heard his words. Her own thoughts were all she could handle. It was over. When she had looked at Brandon after the judge had read the verdict, she had seen him busily trying to comfort a stunned and outraged Serena, who had burst into dramatic, angry tears. He had been too busy, Cully had noted, even to come over to her table and deliver the customary congratulations. He was going to carry a grudge, she told herself sadly. Hadn't she learned what men were like after Dick? Hadn't she learned that even the best of them thought that all women had a proper place—a place that didn't threaten men?

She sat in her chair, shredding yellow tissues made soft by her tears, dropping the pieces into the wastepaper basket next to her.

She had thought that Brandon was different. Different! If he had been so different, she thought angrily, why hadn't he called her after she had left him that note, pouring out her heart? No, there was no use trying to reason any of it out. He didn't care . . . perhaps had never cared. She had been a fool.

Her intercom buzzed. She looked at it as she would have looked at an intruding enemy. She didn't want to talk to anyone. She had told June that. Her eyes, she realized, were red-rimmed, and she was too busy feeling sorry for herself to put up with anyone else. Why couldn't everyone just leave her alone?

But the buzzing persisted. She ignored it. Suddenly her door flew open.

"Sir, you can't—" June protested, trying to bar his way.

"I already have!" the voice thundered, its angry owner banging the door shut behind him.

Brandon!

"Wha-what are you doing here?" Cully asked, trying to sound impersonal. Her voice shook.

"Trying to corner you, obviously," he said. His blue eyes snapped with annoyance.

Cully rose, putting up her hands to keep him at bay until she got her words out. Another shredded tissue fell from her lap. "Look, I know you're angry, but I had to do what I had to do."

"Of course I'm angry," he retorted. "When I finally extricated myself from Serena and her Academy Award performance, you had bolted from the courtroom."

"I hardly bolted," she sniffed. God, why did she have to look like such a mess? He'd think she was crying over him. He'd think the truth, she realized ruefully.

"You bolted," he insisted.

"Well, I don't see where you'd care anyway," she told him with an indifferent shrug of her shoulders, trying to retain some tiny particle of pride. She didn't want him thinking that she was heartbroken over losing him, not when he obviously wasn't heartbroken over losing her.

"What the hell are you babbling about? You're beginning to sound like a typical woman."

"Well, maybe I am," she shot back defensively.

"Typical? You?" He laughed mockingly. "I wouldn't have been attracted to you if you were typical. Maybe I'm a snob, but I wanted someone a little different."

"Uh-huh." It was clear that she didn't believe him. She folded her arms across her chest, turning away from him and looking out the window. The panoramic view of the city that lay before her was lost on Cully. It was just that she couldn't bear looking into his eyes any longer. "That's why you didn't call after our weekend," she said bitterly. She couldn't keep the words from her lips. But once they were said, she was sorry. How could he help but see her hurt?

Brandon placed two strong hands on her shoulders, holding her captive. "I didn't call because I decided to give you that fighting chance."

"What?"

"Hold your tongue, counselor, for just one minute. We all know what you can do with words," he said lightly. His tone was getting more patient as his anger appeared to dissipate. "After I read your note, I realized how important it was for you to try to win, and I knew that if I saw you right before the trial, maybe your reflexes wouldn't be so sharp. So I bowed out temporarily."

Slowly Cully turned around, wonder in her eyes. Could she believe him? Could she possibly hope that he was still interested in her, even after what had happened that day?

"You threw the case for me?" she asked, wanting to grasp the entire meaning of his statement.

"Oh, no, nothing that altruistic. I wasn't about to capitulate to you. I was going to give you a run for your money—or theirs, so to speak. But for once," he said, looking down into her face, his expression almost tender, "I wanted my 'worthy opponent' to have a good chance at it as well. It was the only honorable thing to do. Remember, I told you I was honorable," he teased.

"Then you're not angry . . . about losing?" she pressed.

"I don't like losing," he told her honestly, then murmured, "especially something that's very important to me." He wasn't talking about the case any longer, she thought happily.

Brandon's hands were resting on either side of her supple hips. Almost independently, they drew concentric circles on her sides, reaching up higher as he spoke until both hands were just beneath her breasts. "I'll admit that at first I did try to unnerve you. Having a little extra ammunition never hurts. But I've fallen in love with you, Yvette Culhane—with the proud tilt of your head, with your staunch belief in principles, with your wonderful, sweet mouth." As if to emphasize his words, he kissed her, his mouth just lightly brushing hers.

She swallowed hard, dazed. "But you lost to me . . ."

"So I did. And," he chuckled, "as far as I know, my manhood is still intact. Of course," he continued loftily, "we'll have to check that out soon, just to make sure." His deep chuckle died in his throat as both his manner and his words became serious. He lifted her chin, forcing her eyes to meet his. "I'm proud of you for facing up to me. Don't you see?" he asked. "If I had wanted a doormat to share my life with, I could have gotten married long ago. I'm fussy. I want a complete woman, not one who plays silly games she thinks will placate me. I'm too much of a man for that. And I want too much of a woman to be satisfied with anything less. I want you," he ended, his voice thick with a sudden surge of desire.

"Share your life with?" Cully echoed.

His smile turned into a pleased grin. "Knew you'd catch the key phrase. Yes, share my life with. You can still keep whatever name you feel will help your practice," he told her. "You can call yourself 'potato' if you choose." Cully tried to suppress a wild giggle. "But I want you to be my wife, no matter what you call yourself. Court cases may come and go, but you're the one thing I don't want to lose, understood, counselor?"

"Understood." She thought she would burst with happiness as he hugged her to him.

"Good," Brandon announced, then released her. He walked to the door and flipped the lock, then, as Cully watched, puzzled, he came back to her desk and depressed the intercom switch. "June," he said, "hold all calls."

"I already told her to do that," Cully said, a smile spreading on her lips.

"It never hurts to reinforce things," Brandon replied, coming toward her and sweeping her into his arms.

"And what are you doing?" she asked, trying to keep her voice steady as Brandon kissed the side of her neck, bringing her skin alive with anticipation as he pinned her against her desk.

"I'm reinforcing things—like the way I feel about you."

Cully melted into his kiss, and it was only after a long burst of background noise that she realized her buzzer had gone crazy. She withdrew her lips from Brandon and leaned backward over her desk. With trembling fingers she hit the intercom button.

"Yes?" she whispered. The force of his kiss had taken all her breath away.

"Are you all right?" June demanded sharply. "When *he* told me to hold all calls I wondered just what was going on." She sounded ready to call out the marines to come to Cully's aid.

"I'm terrific," Cully said, releasing the switch and beaming up at Brandon.

"You bet you are," he said huskily. "And you're going to get a chance to prove it every day of our life together."

"You set high standards," Cully breathed as Brandon began removing her clothes.

"Only for people I know can live up to them," he assured her, his eyes no longer on her face but on the swell of her breasts, which rose and fell sharply with her excited breathing.

"Brandon, we can't," Cully protested against his mouth. Her own hands gave the lie to the statement as they undid his vest and shirt. The feel of his chest was so wonderful, so reassuring. Her cool fingers raked along his skin, just as his did along her panty line. Her skirt rested in a circle about her shoes.

"Oh, yes, we can," he replied. "My manhood, remember? We're supposed to see if it's intact." He said the words against her face as he addressed each part of her with smoldering, tantalizing kisses.

Cully stood pressed against him, a force greater than her sense of propriety compelling her on. "Your manhood, I'm happy to inform you, seems to be very much intact." A mischievous grin that matched his own was on her face. But it melted away as Brandon lifted her up in his strong arms and gently deposited her on her sofa. The cool leather chilled her skin, but within a moment the feel of cool leather was miles away from her mind as she strove to absorb the gratifying feel of his magnificent body.

As Brandon lay over her, the weight of his body teasing her, he paused for a moment, cupping her small face and framing it in his sturdy hands. "I love you, counselor, love you like I've never loved anyone before in my whole life. It's an all-encompassing love, Evie. I love you more than the principles of law that mean so much to me . . . love you more than I ever loved Marvin."

Cully's eyes opened wide. "Marvin?"

"My collie. Had him for thirteen years." His face was solemn, but his eyes danced.

An irrepressible giggle broke loose and she found that for a moment, despite her state of undress and her very horizontal, compromising position, she couldn't stop laughing.

"What are you laughing at? Marvin was the best friend I ever had . . . until you happened along."

"And I don't come with fleas," she quipped.

"Marvin didn't have fleas," Brandon corrected, feigning indignation. "He also didn't smell this good," he told her, his voice lowering as well as his face. Brandon pressed his lips against her neck and all laughter died away as passion rose up in its stead to claim her.

Ecstasy, endless ecstasy, joined their souls as their bodies merged so perfectly. Beyond the waves of passion, Cully felt an exhilarating happiness. Never again would she have to fear standing up for what she believed in, never again would she have to worry about how her actions would affect a man's ego. The man who had chosen to live out his life with her had proven to be above that, and their love had been tried and proven to be true. Cully had never heard a sweeter verdict in her life.

The afternoon sun cast its rays through her window when Cully and Brandon finally faced one another fully dressed again. The joy of their lovemaking still held her in its grip as she watched him flip open the lock with one hand while drawing her against him with the other.

"C'mon, let's go tell my future son what we've decided," he urged, then grinned down into her contented face. "And then we'll go to my place."

"Oh?" she asked, snuggling into the hollow of his arm, loving the feeling of being so close to him. "Why?"

He stopped dead in his tracks, as if mystified that she should even ask. "Why, to check up on my manhood again, of course. These things bear close watching, you know."

Cully's gentle laughter filled the hall as they walked out of her office together.